DOORWAY
THROUGH TIME

LIN HARBERTSON

authorHOUSE®

AuthorHouse™
1663 Liberty Drive
Bloomington, IN 47403
www.authorhouse.com
Phone: 1-800-839-8640

Published by AuthorHouse 11/28/2012

ISBN: 978-1-4772-9345-4 (sc)
ISBN: 978-1-4772-9344-7 (hc)
ISBN: 978-1-4772-9343-0 (e)

Library of Congress Control Number: 2012922207

The people come and go.
The generations, marriages, children, all come and go.
Only the land remains.

It was as she was leaving the brightly lit off-license, with its polished wooden countertop, wrinkling her nose at the sour scent of wine and beer, that Alison overheard the tail end of a whispered conversation between the proprietor and his wife.

"Two bottles of the best bubbly this week! Is he out of town again?"

"I'm sure he is—that dreadful husband of hers. Always leaving her all by herself. Poor woman. I hope she's going to be all right. Do you know what their neighbor Mrs. Allan says?"

Are they talking about me? she wondered. *Is that what people are thinking?*

But as Alison made her way through the northern England town of Roystone that bright autumn morning, she couldn't know that something was about to happen that would change her quiet life forever. She walked briskly, hurrying to find out if her favorite shop, the art gallery, was open. It always seemed to be closed for a half-day holiday that changed unexpectedly each week. She suspected that Mr. Grimes, the owner, spent most of his time at the Roystone races.

As she approached the art gallery—breathing a sigh of relief when she saw it was open—an oil painting in the window caught her eye. She crossed the street with a sense of anticipation. Such an oil painting; it depicted a hunting scene in which a woman was jumping a chestnut horse, sidesaddle, across a fence. Waiting for her on the far side of the fence was a man dressed in a red hunting jacket. He was riding a large black horse, and in the background were the rest of the hunt, galloping after the hounds. It was called *Gone Away*. As she stood gazing at the painting, she noticed her reflection in the glass. The face that had looked so serious was now smiling back at her. *Why not?* she thought. *Why not?*

Alison opened the door, listening to the tinkling sound of the bell as she inhaled the fragrances of oils and dust. The little shop was silent and a little dark, its uneven walls covered with artwork of all different sizes, shapes, and colors. Mr. Grimes was sitting under a bright light in the farthest corner, studying a watercolor.

"Mr. Grimes," she began, "how much is it? The picture in the window?" She held her breath.

"Oils are always more expensive, Mrs. Simons," said Mr. Grimes, peering over his glasses. The painting was on consignment and had sat in his shop for three or four years—the owners were asking such an exorbitant price. He sighed before telling Alison the price, wondering how high she was willing to go. He decided to raise it slightly to give himself room to negotiate with her and then felt guilty when she immediately accepted it without question.

Alison closed her mind to the amount she was writing on the check. *What am I thinking? I can't afford this kind of expenditure.* Her broker had delivered the bad news to her the previous week. She had lost half of her capital in the latest stock market crash. Still, she was undeterred.

"I'm glad you bought it," Mr. Grimes said. "I've always liked this painting. I expect it will think it's going home. Would delivery tomorrow morning be all right?"

Alison nodded and then looked questioningly at him. "Going home?"

"Oh yes, this painting has quite a history. It's somehow connected with your house, although I've forgotten the details," he said as he gave her a receipt. "But then, anything old is bound to have a history, isn't it?"

"How old?" she asked.

"Probably painted about 1850 or so."

Alison looked at her watch. She was torn. She longed to ask him for more details, but she was out of time that morning. "I'll come back tomorrow," she said. "Perhaps you'll have remembered something by then. Thank you, Mr. Grimes."

As she was leaving, he opened the door for her and inquired, "How's the new book?"

"I think now it will do very well," she replied, looking at the painting once again and smiling.

He smiled back at her and had a sudden thought. "Are you going to the races next Saturday?"

"Of course," she replied.

As Alison drove home, her thoughts were on the painting—on the woman riding sidesaddle and the man waiting for her. Were they lovers? Was their love the kind that lasted forever, something she wrote about in her novels? She sighed heavily and gripped the steering wheel a little tighter. She and her husband, Jack, had become silent strangers. Was it because of her success? Was he jealous? At first, it had seemed so exciting—the home in the north of Yorkshire, a home that she remembered so well from her childhood. She had been able to purchase it with the royalties from her first successful novel, *Murder by Moonlight*, but now she wasn't sure the move from London had been such a good idea.

Inexplicably, Jack had been furious when the book had proved to be very popular. "You didn't tell me it was a sordid romance!" he'd stormed at her.

"It's not sordid; it's romance!" she had shouted back at him. "And I asked you to read it many times!"

"I don't like the way people look at me in this town. It's because of your books. I know it is. Where do you get your ideas?"

From my imagination, she thought. Oh yes, she'd always had a brilliant imagination but had taken it for granted … until lately. Now, it was silent; no ideas flooded her mind with vivid pictures. There was just emptiness. No matter how hard she tried to open it, the doorway to her imagination was closed, almost as if it were locked. Her publisher was calling her weekly, reminding her of her contract, beseeching her for "just a rough draft of something new," but her mind stubbornly refused to cooperate.

Her imagination had lain quiet until this morning, when she glimpsed that painting in the shop window. Already, whispers were beginning, curling at the edges of her consciousness. She hoped that by the afternoon, some of them would have coalesced into something with which to pique the curiosity of the newspaper reporters from the *Roystone Herald*. They were to interview her that afternoon, and she already was late from making a quick run to town to buy champagne. "Now, Alison," her publisher had encouraged her. "Tell them something—tell them anything—and if you can't think of anything, open a bottle of something expensive. The article will remind the public of your last book. Sales are down. It's been three years you know."

How well she knew! But now, maybe she would be able to write again. Alison threaded her way through the narrow streets of Roystone, carefully avoiding the throngs of shoppers enjoying the unexpected warm weather. How lucky she was to have found such a magnificent painting. She knew it was going to look perfect in her living room. Her heart sang, thinking about it.

The road meandered through the town, following the course of the river, before it turned to cross the bridge and continue toward her home at the top of the hill. The two-story house, made of cut stone, stood well back from the road, and the entire property, twenty-five acres, was surrounded by a stone wall.

The wrought-iron gate to the property was open, lying on its side and unattended. *I really must get it fixed*, Alison thought as she parked her car. Her neighbors had installed electric gates with security codes ("You can't be too careful, my dear"), but then she forgot about the open gate, admiring the sycamore trees that lined both sides of the driveway. She loved this house. As a child, she had spent her summers here with her grandparents, riding horses, enjoying her freedom, and forgetting all about her dreaded boarding school.

All was quiet; the reporters had not yet arrived. Alison opened the front door and stepped inside. The front door once had opened directly into the kitchen, but now it opened onto an elegant entryway, with doors leading to the kitchen, the living room, a bathroom, and her study. She walked into the large kitchen, poured herself a glass of milk, and gulped half of it down. Mrs. Crocket had left a plate of scones for her on the table, and now Alison sliced a couple of them and spread strawberry jam on top before checking her answering machine. Several messages were from people who either wanted to buy her books or sell her their horses, and there was yet another from her publisher, a dynamic gentleman whose nickname was Beaky. "My dad owns the firm, B and K Publishing," he had informed her, "and he has always been known as BK, hence my name. When he retires, I shall be BK." They had met once, and she had been most impressed with him and dazzled by his turn of speech but hadn't realized until she signed the contract with what tenacity he would expect her to stick to its terms. "How's the new book coming along?" the recorded voice asked. "Not well," she muttered in reply. "Not well"—but now there was hope.

Munching on the scones, Alison put the champagne in the refrigerator and set out plenty of crackers and cheese, glasses, and paper plates. Then she hid the rest of the scones—they were her favorites. She checked her watch—the reporters were late—and then, while she was waiting, she sat down at the table with her laptop computer and swiftly tapped out a description of the painting. *What did Mr. Grimes mean that the painting was going home?* she wrote.

Alison shivered. The house felt cold; it always did at this time of the year. She turned on the central heat and lit the gas fire in the living room to take the edge off the damp. Then she stepped outside the front door to wait for the reporters. The early morning sunshine was fading, and dark clouds were gathering behind the sycamores. *What a shame. Too bright too early*, she thought.

As it turned out, only one reporter, Jennifer Standing, arrived. Jennifer was a big fan of Alison's books, and she had a horse that she was having a problem with.

"Before we get started, can you help me? Everyone says you are so good at helping difficult horses, Mrs. Simons. I just don't know what to do," Jennifer said. "I have a new horse, and he's gaited. I always wanted one, but he doesn't seem to know how to keep the running walk steady. He goes faster and faster until he's unbalanced, and then he throws his head in the air and almost falls down."

They spent several hours drinking tea instead of champagne, eating the cheese and crackers, and talking over horse remedies. Alison felt so comfortable with Jennifer that she brought out the scones and strawberry jam to share. Then Alison posed for photographs, and by the time the subject of the new book came up, she had a suitable answer.

"It's a historical, romantic thriller," she said, "with a beautiful heroine, an old house"—and then a new idea struck her—"and of course, a murder."

Jennifer nodded as she took notes. Her next question took Alison by surprise. "Mrs. Simons, what made you start writing books?"

Alison poured herself another cup of tea and slowly sat back in her chair. "Why did I start writing? I don't know, really. A degree in journalism and an overactive imagination, perhaps." The truth, which she didn't care to share, was that as Jack spent less and less time at home, she had created imaginary worlds for herself—and she had discovered that other people enjoyed reading about them.

Jennifer thanked Alison profusely for her time and all her advice. After she left, Alison breathed a sigh of relief and then rushed up the winding staircase to her bedroom, taking the stairs two at a time. The house originally had five bedrooms, but the fifth bedroom had been converted into a bathroom and a walk-in linen cupboard by the previous owner, Mrs. Brown. When it still was a bedroom, it had been kept locked. "You stay out of there," her grandfather had said, frightening her with the severity of his voice.

It was not a fancy house but very comfortable, with its wooden floors and wood-beamed ceilings. All the rooms had large windows and grand views, either of the stable that lay behind the house or the sycamores and the valley in the front.

Alison changed into her riding clothes and ran down the stairs to the scullery, on the far side of the kitchen. The two parts of the house were connected by an old wooden door. The scullery had a stone floor and a sink, and she found it most useful for storing her shoes, boots, heavy winter coats, and assorted riding equipment. No matter when she opened the door, she always could detect the scent of the apples that had once been stored there, long ago. She pulled on her riding boots before walking quickly out to the stable to visit Captain, an old brown thoroughbred that had been with her for many years. She thought of Captain as a trusted friend.

He whinnied a greeting to her. "I know you're lonesome," Alison said. "It's a lovely day. Let's go for a ride." She had permission to ride on the neighboring properties as long as she closed the gates and didn't disturb the crops or the livestock, and she cherished this privilege. They cantered happily along the edges of fields full of sheep, through small copses of oak trees, and stopped at the top of a hill to admire the view. Below were more fields and more sheep, and far away they could just make out the end of the land and the beginning of the sea.

It was almost dark by the time they reached the gate and home.

Alison fed Captain before she went down to the house, giving him grain as well as a flake of hay. "It was a perfect afternoon," she said to him giving him a hug. "You are my favorite horse of all time."

She had already eaten her dinner when she heard the front door slam. She knew it was Jack. He was home late from work as usual. His office was a large brick two-story building on the outskirts of the town. It had been used years ago as a workhouse, and with its few, small, heavily barred windows and narrow chimneys rising out of the steep roof, it always reminded Alison of something out of a gloomy Victorian novel.

She stood watching him, almost apprehensively, as he entered the kitchen. She could never tell what kind of mood he would be in and searched his face for clues. She noticed that his dark hair now was streaked with more gray than she remembered, and the lines on his face were more deeply etched than ever. For a moment, she had the oddest feeling—it was as if she were looking at the face of a complete stranger. He was older than her by ten years, and since moving to Roystone, his silences made him seem more remote than ever.

"Busy day?" she asked him tentatively.

"Of course. I ate already," he replied and then sat down at the kitchen table to work on a schematic for a security system he was designing. "The security system I'm working on is for this house," he announced suddenly. "If I have to live way out in the middle of nowhere, I want to be safe."

Alison sighed; Jack was obsessed with security. She wished they could talk together the way they used to. She found his presence to be even more depressing than usual and decided she didn't want to tell him about the painting. She put his dinner in the refrigerator, cleaned up the kitchen, and said, "I'm off to bed, Jack. There are plenty of snacks in the refrigerator if you want anything." He ignored her. *As usual*, she thought.

She sighed as she climbed into bed, trying to think about a plot for her new novel. Sometimes those ideas she had before she fell asleep were her best. But this night, her last thoughts before she fell asleep were of the painting. She tried to picture it on the wall of the living room. She remembered to put her mobile phone on the charger before she turned out the light, and she fell asleep long before Jack came to bed.

When she awoke, the sunlight was streaming in through the window, and she was alone. *What time did Jack get up?* she wondered. *Is he was deliberately avoiding me? Why can't he spend more time at home?* Then she realized that even if he did, they would have nothing to talk about. Certainly not her horses, or her books, or anything else. *Is this to be my life now?* she thought sadly.

After quickly dressing, Alison went out to the stable to feed Captain. He was pacing restlessly. "I'm sorry I sold your friend," she said. "We'll just have to find you another, won't we?" She sang him a nonsense song as she fed him a flake of hay and cleaned out his stall. Just being around her horse gave her a feeling of peace and contentment. She leaned on the pitchfork she was using to clean the stall as she stood looking out over the familiar view of the valley. She remembered her distress at the sudden death all those years ago of her much loved grandmother and the property being put up for sale.

"Please can we buy it?" she had begged her mother. "Please?"

"Who wants to live way out there?" her mother had replied. "In that old house? It would cost a fortune to make it livable."

No one else in the family had been interested in the house or the twenty-five acres of land, so it had been sold to a Mrs. Brown. *Maybe Mother was right*, she thought. Jack certainly complained bitterly about living "out in the sticks," but Alison reveled in the peace that she had found. She felt close to the land where her father's family had lived for many years, close to the memories of her grandparents. Now, she could keep her horses at home instead of boarding them, and there were miles of riding trails to explore.

The sound of a van laboring up the hill disturbed her thoughts, and she remembered that the painting was going to be delivered that morning. She gave Captain a final pat. "See you later, old boy," she said. "Be good now, and no jumping over that fence."

The van pulled up at the door and two young men carried the painting into the house. The room was large, with white walls, a high ceiling with exposed brown beams, and a wooden floor covered with rugs. On one side was a fireplace, and next to it were French doors with soft apple-green curtains that opened onto a garden.

"Where do you want us to put it, luv?" one of the men asked her.

"Here," she replied. "Please hang it here, opposite the fireplace."

Once on the wall, the painting looked as if it belonged there—as if it had always been there—so well did it blend in with its surroundings. One of the men, whose name was Bob, said, "This painting used to be in this room on this very wall. I remember seeing it at the sale."

Alison startled. "Sale?" she asked.

"Yes," said Bob. "When Mrs. Brown passed away, some cousin inherited it all from her, and he put everything up for sale. Didn't you know? Her son was in the army, and he were killed. She were a grand lass. Lived up here all by herself. She loved that painting. Said it were something special!"

The furniture and paintings had not been included when Alison purchased the house, but then, she had made an offer over the phone without seeing it, as soon as she had heard it was on the market. Suddenly, she couldn't wait for the men to leave. They sensed her impatience and departed hurriedly, with cheerful good humor.

Once she was alone, she inhaled the presence of the painting that filled the room. *How it belongs here!* Then the fragrance of old roses came to her, and she opened the glass French doors onto the garden and saw, in her imagination, flowers there instead of the grass and shrubs.

What a lovely idea, Alison thought. She fetched her laptop, sat on her favorite chair, found the website of a local nursery, and immediately ordered rose bushes—roses that would continuously bloom. She ordered just a few to get started. She would ask the gardener for more ideas. *Can I afford a gardener now?* she wondered. *What a depressing thought.* Then she looked at the painting and felt lucky that she'd found it and was able to bring it home. She thought about the people in it and the type of lives they might have led. She spent the rest of the day happily letting her mind wander over the possibilities of a plot for her novel. She was far away, daydreaming, when she heard the front door open. *Jack! Surely he will be pleased.*

"Jack, Jack, come and see. Look at the painting I found," she called out. She ran to the front door and took his arm. Reluctantly, he allowed her to lead him into the living room. "Isn't it magnificent? Do say you like it, and I've had a marvelous idea for the garden."

Jack stared at the painting, shaking his head. "I've seen at least a hundred of these paintings since we moved north," he said flatly. "Roystone seems full of endless pictures of horses, jumping over endless fences."

Alison's enthusiasm would not be dampened. She opened the French doors and walked outside, calling back to him, "We could plant some roses, here and here. What do you think? We could put some tables and chairs out here and sit to watch the sunsets. Wouldn't that be delightful?"

Jack ignored the rose idea completely. He waited until she was back in the room with him and then walked over to the French doors, closed them tightly, and locked them. "We can't be too careful, my dear, can we?" he said.

Alison crossed her fingers hopefully as she sat in her favorite chair next to the fire. "Jack," she began quietly, knowing her next words would take him by surprise. "I've been invited to a writer's club monthly dinner next week, and we've been invited to a racing club dinner too. Please go with me."

"So sorry, my dear, not possible right now," he replied, refusing to look at her. "I'm leaving on another business trip very early tomorrow. I'm off to New York for a big security installation. I have a new business phone number, too. I've put it on the kitchen table for you."

She watched him as quickly he turned to leave, and she heard the familiar thump-thump as he dragged his suitcase out of the cupboard in the bedroom. Alison sighed; all her happiness had fled. Jack had succeeded in putting a damper on her high spirits even faster than usual. He was going out of town again. What was going on with him? It had been such a long time since they had done anything together; they were living completely separate lives. Was it her fault? *Winners and losers,* she thought. *Winners and losers. Easier to pick a long-shot winner at a horse race than to find a man one could love forever.* Yet that was exactly what she did want.

She thought about the horse that had been offered to her, one that she had been unable to resist—a racehorse that refused to run. She would make her final decision on Saturday after the last race. Colossus, they called him. Would he turn out to be a winner or a colossal mistake? All her instincts told her that he was going to be a winner. What a gamble life was. She drank a glass of wine and watched the painting in the light from the fire. How the shadows passed across it, making the horses move. She almost fell asleep in her chair, watching them.

2

When Alison awoke with a start the next morning, the bed next to her was cold and empty, and she knew that Jack was gone already, without even a kiss good-bye. *When was the last time he kissed me or held me? Come to think of it, when was the last time I wanted him to?* It was then she heard a rattling sound as something hit the window. She put on her dressing gown and looked outside. There was her neighbor, Mr. Murphy, looking up at her. He had a halter in one hand and a handful of gravel in the other. She opened the window, flinching at the cold air on her face.

"You could have knocked at the front door," she called out.

"I did. No one answered. It's that blasted horse of yours again, Mrs. Simons!" he shouted. "Down at my place, trampling my vegetables and upsetting the mares. Should be locked up."

"Sorry!" Alison shouted back. "I'll be right over." She dressed hurriedly, fetched a halter and rope, and ran down the hill to collect Captain. The trouble had begun a month ago when she had been offered a price she couldn't refuse for his companion. Captain was lonely now and had opened the gate to go looking for company. Sure enough, there he was at Murphy's place, leaning over a fence, sweet-talking a pretty mare. Mr. Murphy owned several Cleveland bays and did not want his mares, all in foal, disturbed.

"Come on, you old devil," said Alison, holding out a handful of grain from her pocket. He came to her, whickering. She slipped the halter over his brown head and scrambled onto his back, using the fence as a mounting block. From this high vantage point, she could see the devastation in the vegetable garden. Captain had been looking for carrots and had not only opened the gate onto Murphy's property but also had jumped the fence into the vegetable garden. In order to avoid another meeting with Murphy and his wrath, she decided to leave by the back gate and go home the long way.

Captain's shoes echoed on the blacktopped road as they passed Ben Jones's place, the dealer. It was then that she noticed the colt. He was trotting in a field alongside the road—gray neck arched, black mane and tail flying. It seemed as if he had wings on his heels, for his feet looked as if they barely touched the ground. Ben was out feeding his animals, and Allison hallooed him.

"Is that a new horse?" she asked, pointing.

"Yes," he said, walking over to her. "He's for sale. Rising three, registered Welsh pony, dog gentle." She noticed again that his voice had the soft lilt of a Welshman. "Just needs castrating that's all. Used to belong to old man Johnson that died last week. Nothing you couldn't afford, Mrs. Simons," he said. She wondered if he'd raised the price to her. She was sure he had. He probably thought he deserved whatever he could get her to pay. "Would you catch the colt for her so I can look at him closer?" She observed the colt's honest eye and elegant shape to the head. Without a second thought, she bought him. "Has he a name?" she asked.

"Samson" replied Ben, his back toward her now, and when he turned, she saw a gleam in his dark brown eyes and an odd expression on his face.

"I'll pick him up tomorrow morning then," she said, ignoring the feeling in her guts that usually presaged trouble. She liked the look of this pony. She knew Captain would be glad of the company, but already she was fancying herself on the colt's back, feeling the power of his body beneath her, the smoothness of his paces, his long legs extending to produce those ground-covering strides.

The next morning, Alison rode Captain down to Ben Jones's farm. He was ready and waiting for her with a halter and lead rope on the colt.

"I had the farrier out to him earlier this morning," he said.

She thought she detected a furtive note to his voice. She also noticed a new cut over the colt's nose and a new anxious look in his eye. For an instant, she wondered at the wisdom of purchasing another horse from Ben. She took hold of the lead rope and prepared to pony the colt home, wondering what to expect, but she was pleasantly surprised. He walked alongside Captain very quietly, and they arrived home with no problems.

A rare picture he looked the next morning. Alison had turned him out in the small pasture the night before, and he was playing in the sunshine, rearing and dancing. She thought she'd tie him up, brush him, and pick up his feet before the vet arrived. Without thinking, she tied him to a nearby post and ran her hands down his near side front leg. It was lucky she had picked a stout post, because he set back on that rope hard, reared up, and fell over on his side. She was untying the rope to let him get up, when suddenly, without any warning, he lunged at her with teeth bared. Instinctively, she ducked behind the post. He gave a sort of squeal and came after her on his hind legs. For an instant, all she could see was the gray of his underbelly and those sharp hooves, pointing at her chest. She rolled aside, grabbing a chain from her pocket—one she had put there "just in case" that very morning—and aimed it at his head. It struck him a blow on the nose, but he whirled around and came at her again. Safety over the gate was too many yards away for her to reach easily, but she had to try. Throwing the chain at his head this time and ducking under his hooves, she ran for it. The colt was after her in an instant, and she didn't believe she would have escaped if the vet, Dr. Harry Hastings, hadn't hit him a resounding blow on the forehead with his stick. The blow stopped him in his tracks and made him regard them both with considerable respect. Harry waved the stick in front of the colt's nose, and the colt turned and trotted off to the far end of the field, to observe them carefully, from a distance.

Alison heaved a huge sigh of relief and leaned against the gate for a moment to recover her breath and her wits. "Harry, I'm so glad to see you," she finally said. "I didn't hear you drive up."

"Good thing I arrived in time. Are you okay?"

Alison reflected that if there were ever any trouble, Harry was the perfect man to have at one's side. He was young and strong and so gentle that all the animals instinctively trusted him. He had bright blue eyes; fair, curly hair; and a mouth that, in curving upward, seemed to be laughing at the world. *Perhaps it was those blue eyes of his that had earned him a reputation. Probably just gossip,* she thought, as he worked alone. He had always been most courteous with her. She liked his steadiness and the fact that he was always on time.

"Who sold you that brute?" he asked. When she told him, his usually cheerful expression faded, and his mouth tightened into a straight line. After a moment, he looked at her. "Did he hurt you?" he asked.

"No, I think I'm okay," Alison replied, brushing the dirt from her clothes and hoping she looked stronger than she felt.

"You want him gelded? Then let's go and get him," Harry said quietly.

Together, they cornered the colt at the end of the field. While Alison grabbed the dangling halter rope, Harry slipped in the first injection, and in a minute, Samson began to sway. Harry went to the Land Rover for his instruments while Alison moved the colt away from the fence. The second shot dropped him to the ground. Alison wrapped a sack over and under his head to protect his eyes. "Be sure to get it all," she said.

"Yes, I know what you mean. Don't worry," said Harry.

The colt's upper rear leg was hobbled and pulled forward to clear the operating area.

"Keep pulling on that rope," he instructed. A minute later, it was over. "I took plenty of tissue above," he said. "He should be a lot safer for you to handle now." He gave the horse two more shots in the neck and a mouthful of wormer. "All done."

As they waited for the colt to wake up, they admired the day. It was warm, with a touch of autumn in the air—the haziness that makes that season different from any other.

"You have a lovely view from here."

"Yes," Alison sighed. "It's a good life." *If I live long enough to enjoy it,* she thought. Her luck almost had run out that morning.

They looked out over the green of the valley, with its silver trail of a river winding its way lazily to the sea. The homes in the town of Roystone dotted the riverbanks and in the distance, they could just see the racecourse.

"I always loved this house when I was a child," she said, almost absentmindedly.

"I didn't know you lived here then," he said in surprise. "Were you related to old Mrs. Forster?"

"She was my grandmother."

"Your grandmother?" he said. "So ... you must be Alison Forster. And we never met."

"Perhaps we did. At a horse show, I went to lots of them in the summers."

"And I was always showing sheep for my brother," he said, laughing. "Did you know your grandmother's maiden name was Hastings? She was my grandfather's sister."

"So she was." Alison had forgotten. "So that makes us sort of cousins," she said.

"Sort of," said Harry, looking at her thoughtfully.

The colt was coming to now and after several tries, he was on his feet, a little unsteady but awake.

"He'll be all right," said Harry. "Trot him twice a day for fifteen minutes for two weeks, and if he swells up larger than a grapefruit, let me know. Have you a name for him yet?"

"El Tigre," she said. "Tigger for short."

"Appropriate enough," he replied. Then he turned to look at her and said, almost scolding, "How many times have I asked you to let me vet-check them before you put down your money?"

Alison smiled sheepishly. This was the fifth or sixth horse she had purchased in the past three years. She seemed to have a knack for finding them and then reselling them at a profit, but this was the first one that had given her trouble.

"You are taking too many chances," he chastised her. "Especially as you're working with them on your own."

Alison helped Harry pick up the neat pile of blood-soaked cotton and his instruments without saying a word, and then they made their way to the house.

She really owed him big time for saving her life, and to make amends for her admitted foolishness with the colt, she said, "Harry, would you like to stay for lunch? I bought a painting yesterday. I'd like your opinion of it."

"I'd like that," he said with a grin. "And I'd be glad to take a look at your painting. Just let me get cleaned up first. I'll get changed in your scullery, though."

"Come on in when you're ready then." While Harry was putting away his instruments in the Land Rover and washing his overalls and boots with disinfectant, Alison went looking for the apple cider. Passing the mirror in the entryway, she noticed the dirt all over her face and the beginning of a large bruise on her right arm. "Yikes," she said, hastily giving her hands and face a general wash and a polish in the guest bathroom.

Mrs. Crocket, her housekeeper, was in the kitchen. She was older than Alison by some years. She had raised many children, both her own and her sister's, and Alison felt comfortable with her. There was the warm smell of something baking in the oven.

"Mrs. Simons, are you all right?" Mrs. Crocket asked as soon as she saw her. "You're not hurt, are you?"

"I'm all right, thanks to Harry," Alison answered. "He's a lifesaver. I've invited him for lunch and to look at the new painting. I think I'll just go down to the cellar and see if I can find some cider. Is there any apple pie left over?"

"No, you had the last piece yesterday. I've baked some scones—your favorites. They're still hot, and there's cold meat pie and fresh strawberries with cream."

"Sounds yummy. You're a peach," said Alison. Opening the door to the wine cellar, she headed down into its cool depths. She couldn't find any apple cider but discovered a bottle of Mosel wine and hoped Harry would approve.

Upstairs, she poured him a glass and took it into the living room, where he was closely examining *Gone Away*. He was now wearing a sports jacket and leather shoes to go with his jeans and open-necked shirt, and she thought him to be more good-looking than ever. "Mrs. Crocket invited me in," he said. "You are so blessed that she cooks for you."

"I know. I got really lucky when I first moved here. Well, Harry, what do you think?" she asked him as she handed him the glass of wine. "I think it's really special."

"It's wonderful. There's no signature, but I think I know who the artist was." He raised his eyebrows at the wine. "It's a little early, but why not?" he said. "Here's to your continued good health, Alison. You have excellent taste in paintings as well as horses."

"Thank you. Here's to you, Harry," she said, raising her glass in salute. Blue eyes looked into blue eyes, and she noticed for the first time how tired his eyes looked.

Mrs. Crocket put her head around the doorway. "I've put a lunch out for you both," she said. "I'm off now. I'll be back later in the week."

"Thanks, Mrs. Crocket," said Alison. "Come on, Harry. Let's go eat. I'm starving."

Harry looked approvingly at the table that was set for two in the kitchen and sighed with contentment. "Ben should never have sold you the pony that way," he managed to say, and then there was silence until the meat pie was all gone, and he was working his through a large bowl of scones and strawberries and cream. "But he'll never forgive you for selling that warmblood mare for so much money. I heard you'd promised him right of first refusal if you decided to sell."

She nodded. It was true that she had promised to sell the mare back to Ben.

"And you bought that other filly he wanted right under his nose. I heard that his car broke down that day, and he missed the sale by five minutes. He was furious with you."

No wonder there had been a gleam in Ben's eye, she thought. *But of what? Triumph, maybe?*

"Harry, there was nothing wrong with that colt the day before when I first saw him. But then, yesterday, he had a cut over his nose, and his eyes were really scared. Ben said he'd had the farrier out, and it was when I went to pick up his front leg this morning that he reacted."

"That's quite a grudge he has against you," Harry said, but he offered nothing more, and they finished the rest of the meal in companionable silence.

After finishing his second cup of coffee, Harry looked at his watch. "I have to go," he said reluctantly. "Thanks for an absolutely superb lunch. Mrs. Crocket is a treasure. Promise me you'll call me next time before you buy."

Alison smiled sweetly at him. "I promise," she said. "Are you going to the races on Saturday? I have a horse for you to look at."

"Another one?" said Harry, looking at her curiously. "Then of course I'll be there. Well, I must get back to work. I'm late already." They shook hands at the door but he delayed, unwilling to leave. "Got any hot tips?"

"Not yet, but I will. I always do," said Alison. "And after today, I owe you at least one."

"By the way," he said, "I'll check out the name of the artist with someone I know and get back to you. If it's who I think it is, he used to live in this house. In fact, this house has always had quite a reputation."

Alison's face lit up, and her curiosity knew no bounds when she heard this. She remembered Mr. Grimes talking about the painting "going home."

"What kind of reputation?" she asked. "Would Mr. Grimes know anything?"

"Maybe, but if not, you could always ask Beth Durham. She's the rector's wife."

"Why the rector's wife?"

He checked his watch again and smiled. "She's my aunt. Uh-oh, now I'm really late. See you Saturday. I'll explain everything then. Thanks for lunch," he called out as he ran to his vehicle.

The colt gave Alison no further trouble. She handled him every day, picking up his feet, teaching him to trust her. His manners improved daily, and she began to think that he would turn out to be a good driving pony, something she had always wanted. She saw herself sitting behind him in an elegant two-wheeled cart, while he floated along with that beautiful long stride. She wondered what her best friend, Lisa, would think.

"I'm glad I bought you," she said. "You're much too nice to belong to Ben. You didn't deserve the ill treatment. It's all a question of trust, isn't it? Besides, you're dog-gentle now, and we're going to have some fine times together. You wait and see."

3

Late that afternoon, Alison rode Captain down to the Dog and Duck Inn, an old Tudor-style two-story building, with pointed gables and tall brick chimneys. It was situated about three miles down the hill from her house, at the junction of the main road that led to the town. Behind the inn were stables, and she often left Captain there while she went in for a drink and a meal. It was this that made Roystone so perfectly special. She'd call in advance to let the Pollocks know she was on the way so they'd unlock the back gate for her and her horse.

The Dog and Duck was special too. It was well lit and welcoming, with a dining room that had an open-beamed ceiling and a large fireplace. The walls were hung with stirrups, hunting horns, and pictures of hunting scenes. Years ago, the meets before the hunt were held at the Dog and Duck, and some of the pictures on the walls celebrated this event. Alison always felt at home there, and she thoroughly enjoyed the steak and kidney pudding and apple pie, for which the inn was justly famous.

It was early, but already there were a dozen people eating dinner. She could hear the rise and fall of their conversations, and she could hear the click of the bar billiards being played in the next room. Jennifer Standing, the reporter from the *Roystone Herald*, was sitting on a stool at the bar with her young man, and Alison's neighbors, the Allans, were playing darts with a small crowd that included old man Murphy. He scowled at her but gave her a smile and waved his glass in her direction.

Alison chose a seat at a table where she could wave to anyone she knew who came in the front door. Fred Pollock, the owner—a big, cheerful local man with a red face and a broad Yorkshire accent—came over and asked what she would like to order.

"Steak and kidney pudding—my favorite. Thanks, Fred. A gin and tonic, too, and please ask Mr. Murphy what he would like to drink. It's on me."

"How's the new book coming along?" Fred asked. "The wife's always asking me to ask you about it."

"Slowly," she replied. "The weather's too beautiful to be indoors."

"Ah, it be that," he replied. "An' there'll be plenty of time for writing, come winter."

She agreed with him. Winters had a habit of arriving early and leaving late in Roystone. Then she smiled at Moira, Fred's wife, who was serving drinks behind the bar. Alison hoped it was Moira who read her books and not Fred. After all, she had written them with women in mind.

Moira smiled back and came over with her drink. "Lovely to see you, Mrs. Simons," she said. "Mr. Simons out of town again?" Alison nodded. "Well," said Moira, patting her on the arm, "you're not to worry, luv. You're always welcome here and that lovely horse of yours too. I'll take him a carrot."

Alison smiled her thanks. It was this friendliness that endeared the people of Roystone to her. They were so kind to her, and she found herself enjoying the sound of their voices and speaking with the same soft burr they did—a familiar one, as she used to speak it during her summer holidays from school. "Gone native, have you?" Jack would say with a grimace, but she didn't care. She found the local manner of speech very pleasant. She was drinking her gin and tonic and thinking about the possibility of apple pie for dessert when she noticed Ben Jones walking in the door. "Good evening, Ben," she called out.

He looked surprised to see her. "How's Sampson?" he asked.

"Oh, you mean Tigre? He was gelded yesterday. He's a bit sore, but he'll be okay. I'll have him pulling a carriage in no time." Mentally, she castigated herself for being so foolish as to sell the mare Ben wanted to someone else. If she had been smart, she would have sold her back to Ben, as she had agreed, and kept his good will. But the horse been such a basket case when she bought her and retraining her had been so difficult, that she had decided against it. But ill treating Tigger to get his revenge? She was convinced it was Ben Jones's treatment that had caused the colt to go after her.

Still, she knew Ben would never forgive her for not keeping her word to him. She realized that she had promised, but the mare had been so special, and when her trainer and friend, Lisa T. Jones, offered to buy the mare for enough money to pay off the loan on the new barn, she had accepted. Besides, the mare had so much jumping talent, it would have been wasted on Ben. Of course, the fact that the mare had been on the television recently, winning a huge jumping class in Calgary, Canada, didn't help to assuage his anger.

"I expect you'll include Tigre in your next book then," he sneered.

"Why?" she asked. "Does he have any particular talents that might make him interesting?"

"You'll find out, sooner or later," Ben spat out. "I expect you'll find out about the new shopping center too. The blasted Nightingales'll own the whole town before long! There's a meeting next week. I came to put up flyers." He handed her one and walked away.

She watched him go and then read the flyer in dismay before going to the bar for another gin and tonic. She felt like she needed one. A new shopping center was to be built next to the racecourse. It would have a conference center, an exhibition hall, a showground, and hotels, and a new road would link it all to the motorway. Additional land was to be set aside to build one hundred homes. The land was owned and being developed by Dr. Nightingale, the largest landowner in the county, and there were other local landowners who were investing in the project. Alison's heart sank. She had lived in Roystone for three years and loved the small-town atmosphere, the feeling that they all knew each other. The timelessness of the little town with its narrow, winding streets and stone houses was so unique. She wondered how everyone else was feeling.

"What do you think about this?" she asked Fred, showing him the flyer. "Will you be going to the meeting?"

"I don't think so," he said doubtfully. "You'll have to ask Moira."

"What do you think, Moira?"

"Well, it would bring in more business," opined Moira, "but it'd just bring in more crime. We got plenty of business as it is. We don't need a lot of strangers."

Alison looked around. Moira was right. The place was full of people—people she knew—drinking and talking, playing darts and bar billiards, and eating large platefuls of home-cooked food.

"I agree," Alison sighed. "I love this town just as it is."

"So do I," Moira agreed. Alison ate her steak and kidney pudding and even managed a slice of apple pie before starting for home on Captain. Usually, she enjoyed these rides home in the dusk, with the rustling of the birds in the hedgerows, the owls beginning to fly, the softness of the light, and the sound of Captain's hooves clopping along the road. But tonight she felt alone. Perhaps it was the thought of the new shopping center, and the one hundred new homes, and all the traffic, and all the people. Would Roystone change and become soulless, like so many other towns she knew? Would the town then have a lot of people who were strangers to each other?

She thought of the painting. Ever since she had brought it home, it seemed to always be on the fringes of her mind. She thought of the woman jumping her horse sidesaddle and the man waiting her. What were they to each other? Were they lovers or merely good friends? It was then Alison realized that she was looking for that one special man who would be her soul mate for all eternity. She would meet him and look into his eyes, and they both would know. Then she laughed to herself. That kind of love was only in her romance books, not in real life. What were her chances of finding such a man, even if he existed?

It was after she arrived home and was putting Captain away for the night that ideas for her next book began again to curl around the edges of her mind. She would research the painting and her family history; maybe there was a connection. She would start with Mr. Grimes, then she would visit Harry's aunt, and once there, she could check out the church records. There was always the library—they might have a book on Roystone she could borrow—and failing all that, she would go online and look for information about the history of Roystone.

Maybe Ben would be a character in her next book, rewritten slightly. He had excellent possibilities; the thought cheered her immensely. She gave Captain and Tigger the carrots she had saved for them. "Good night, boys," she said and ran to the house.

The next morning, she drove to the art gallery and asked Mr. Grimes, "Who painted *Gone Away?* I can't find a signature anywhere."

"I wondered if you'd be back," he said. "I'll have to look it up for you, but I think it's a John Trentham. He didn't always sign his paintings. Let's see now … there was something to do with the Hastings family and the Forsters too. I looked that up when the painting was first put on consignment, years ago, but I'm sure Dr. Hastings or his brothers know a lot more than I do. Or you could ask Mrs. Durham—her husband's the rector at the church."

Harry suggested that too, Alison thought. *What's the connection? Why would she know anything about the painting??* Something told her a face-to-face conversation with Harry would be much more interesting than a mere phone call. She drove over to his clinic, but he was out on an emergency call. Frustrated, she decided to try the rector's wife. After parking the car at the bottom of the hill that led to the church, she walked up the winding pathway, past the solemn gravestones. The church was not locked; she pushed open the heavy wooden door and stood in the entryway, looking and remembering. She had not been in this church in years, not since the death of her parents so many years ago. They were both killed instantly when their car was hit by a drunk driver. It had been such a sad time in her life. One moment, she'd had a family, with grandparents and parents, but within a year's time, they were all gone, and she was an orphan.

Alison walked in almost on tiptoe and was enchanted to rediscover the church's simplicity—the stained glass window behind the plain altar, the worn wooden pews, the stone floor, and the wooden roof. She inhaled its sense of timeless silence. She sat down on one of the pews and thought of her years away at school and the endless hours on Sundays spent in church. Was it the peace and love of God that she was seeking?

Someone behind her coughed gently and then said, "It's Norman, in case you were wondering. Built two hundred years after the conquest." It was the rector. He was tall and thin, and there was not one hair on his head. His enormous dark eyes were set in a long narrow skull, and his cheekbones protruded sharply. She remembered hearing that he had been a missionary in Africa for many years and had only recently returned to Roystone. "Nice to meet you at last, Mrs. Simons. I'm Reverend Durham." He had a deep pleasant voice and a firm handshake. "Would you like to come up to the house and meet my wife, Beth? I know she would enjoy meeting you. She reads all of your books." His eyes twinkled at her.

Alison felt her face grow red. *Damn*, she thought. She suddenly felt a little shy. Her books were romance, occasionally lurid, and after all, he was a vicar. Thankfully, he hadn't said that he read them. She was about to decline his offer and make her escape when he said, "Beth's family has lived here for many generations."

Alison smiled, saying, "Thank you. I'd enjoy that very much." She followed him out of the church. "So far, we have been able to leave the church door unlocked," he remarked as he carefully closed the door. "But perhaps that will have to change soon. There is so much vandalism these days. We've had to put everything valuable into storage, and we only bring it out on Sundays, but it does leave the altar looking rather bare." They walked along a pathway lined with rose bushes until they reached the three-story brick home that lay not far from the church. The rector opened the door, and Alison walked into the old house. It was quiet inside, almost like the church, as if it had been there forever. The only sound was the ticking of a grandfather clock. The rector's wife was sewing in a room with large windows that overlooked a walled garden. As soon as she was introduced to Alison, she said, "It's lovely to meet you at last, my dear. Let's have some tea. I've read all your books, you know. Sit here." She moved some newspapers for Alison to sit on a comfortable well-worn chair in front of the fireplace. "Harry said you bought a painting. He thought it might be a John Trentham."

"Yes," Alison said, "I asked Mr. Grimes, and he said to ask you about it. So did your nephew Harry. He's been my vet ever since I moved here."

"Well, Harry's mother was my sister. I expect that's why he said to ask me. I've always kept a lot of the family papers, although Harry's brother John has most of them. I've seen *Gone Away*. Such a grand painting. John Trentham used to live in your house, you know."

Alison thought that was one of the advantages of a small town. Everyone knew everyone else's business. To her, it wasn't being nosy; it was caring about other people.

"Such a scandal it was," Mrs. Durham continued. "My mother told me all about it. John Trentham built the house for his fiancée, Elsie Hastings, but just before the wedding, she married someone else. Her family had given John the land to build her a house. A big disappointment he turned out to be. They never forgave him."

"Why? Why? What did he do?" asked Alison.

"Well … and this is only gossip, now … he was painting a portrait of the mayor's wife and spending a lot of time with her—too much time, as the story goes—and the mayor found out. Elsie's family called off the wedding, and she was married soon after to a Forster. James Forster."

Alison's heart gave a leap. "My maiden name was Forster," she said. She was fascinated and wanted to know more.

"A very good-looking man was John Trentham," said Mrs. Durham. "Tall, with black curly hair. There's a self-portrait of him hanging in the town museum. He never married, but he lived on in that house. He loved to paint animals and birds, as well as portraits. Rumor has it that after Elsie was killed, he disappeared, and he never forgave himself for her death. Always said it was his fault. I think the townspeople thought it was his fault too. Anyway, they blamed him. A man with his reputation? He had to be responsible. He was never seen again, and the house was put up for sale. The Forsters bought it."

"So that's how I inherited the fox painting from my father," Alison said. "That's a John Trentham too."

"Well, then, it would be your great-great-great-grandfather. I'm not sure how many greats, but it was a Forster who bought the house around 1860 or so and everything that was in it. I expect that would include the paintings too."

She begged Mrs. Durham to tell her more about how Elsie died, but Mrs. Durham couldn't remember. After drinking her tea and eating several delicious homemade fruit tarts, Alison regretfully took her leave.

"I didn't realize you were a Forster," Reverend Durham said as he opened the door. "There are quite a few Forsters buried here on the far side of the church. They go way back, you know. I could show you."

"Yes, please. I know my parents and grandparents are there. Is John Trentham there also?"

"Not John Trentham, Mrs. Simons. I don't think anyone knows where he was laid to rest."

The rector led the way along the narrow winding paths around the side of the church, and she carefully followed him. There, next to the outer stone wall, were the graves and headstones of the Forster family. "There are my father and mother, Richard and Eileen," she said sadly, reading the epitaph. "Is it ten years already? I must bring some flowers. Everything is so well tended. Who takes care of them all?" *I should have been here a long time ago*, she thought. She suddenly felt ashamed at her neglect, but her grief and anger at her parents' sudden death had been overwhelming. She hadn't wanted to be reminded of it and even now avoided graveyards. She had always felt them to be strange and unnatural places. She pictured the bodies lying beneath the ground, laid out, row after row after row, going back and back, centuries in time. *Death brought them together, generation after generation, even though they knew each other not in life.* She shuddered. How odd her imagination was.

"Beth takes care of them all," said the rector. "Your grandmother and grandfather, Ellen and Robert Forster, are buried here too. But not your grandfather's siblings. They didn't choose to live in Roystone. Too quiet for them, my wife says. They went away to university, and after that, they moved on. People do that these days, you know, and then they get cremated instead of being laid to rest with their family. There isn't much for young people to do here, and they find it dull. The town has the racecourse but not much else."

"I suppose my father was a Forster who moved on," she mused. "He went into banking. He always said there wasn't much going on here. I expect he was right. I like it, though."

"I'm glad you like it. Of course, the new shopping center will change the town, but perhaps some change is good." Reverend Durham smiled warmly as he asked, "Will we see you on Sunday morning?"

"Yes … perhaps," she said. And then, feeling ungracious, she added, "Sunday, then, and thank you for inviting me, and tell Mrs. Durham thank you."

As she drove home, feeling quietly peaceful, she felt as if she were putting down more roots. She belonged in this town, and it was a good feeling. Since being orphaned at twenty, she had longed to feel that she belonged somewhere. Sadly, her marriage had not filled this place in her heart. Jack was an only child, and she had married him not long after her parents were killed. His family, however, had never accepted her and made her feel like an outsider and unwanted. There always had been an emptiness in her heart, but since moving to Roystone that feeling had begun to melt away. There was a warmth to this town. She felt she belonged here. Buying *Gone Away* had somehow deepened this feeling. She longed to talk to Harry and looked forward to seeing him on Saturday at the races.

It was sunny that Saturday afternoon in early September. For some of the inhabitants of Roystone, it was a time to venture down to the beach, dip their feet in the cold water, and sit on the golden sand. For others, the only place to be on that warm Indian summer afternoon was at the Roystone races.

Being one of the latter group, Alison was leaning idly on the rail that divided the owners from the onlookers, enjoying the sunshine. In the paddock in front of her stood the owners, their friends, and the jockeys. They were standing in small groups, watching the horses being walked around before the 3:30 race. In the stands behind her were all the people who, like her, were here to enjoy this seeming last day of summer.

That was how it seemed to Alison that afternoon as she stood immersed in her surroundings, observing the brightly colored silks of the jockeys, the familiar sounds and smells of the horses and leather, and the disjointed fragments of conversations that wafted over to her on the warm, still air. She had met Jack on an afternoon at the races; now, sadly, he wouldn't dream of going anywhere with her. She sighed. Voices calling her name interrupted her reverie and turning, she found Fred and Moira Pollock looking at her with broad smiles on their faces.

"Hello," she said. "How's the Dog and Duck Inn? Managing without you for the afternoon?"

"It's Moira's birthday today," said Fred.

"It's a wonderful day for a birthday," Alison remarked.

"Made him promise to bring me to the races," Moira said, "and I'm glad he did. What do you think of my hat?"

Alison admired the creation that was large and blue and decorated with tiny plastic oranges. "Very elegant," she said.

"We're off to drink champagne," said Moira, her round face pink with pleasure, "and be waited on for a change. Go on—ask my age."

"Oh, Moira, I couldn't. Mm-m-m ... thirty five?" said Alison.

"Don't I wish," Moira said. "I'll never see thirty-five again, nor forty-five neither. But whatever's left, we're going to enjoy, aren't we, Fred?"

"Every minute," he said vehemently. "Join us for a drink later if you'd like to." Still smiling, the couple sailed away.

Alison found herself envying their happiness, wishing that she too had someone to love, someone with whom to share her life.

She was facing the stands now, and on her right, close to the rail of the course, she could see the bookies. Each one had his name in big letters on a sign above his head. Many were dressed flamboyantly, as if each were vying for the attention of the race-goers, and each had a tic-tac man who now and then waved his arms in frantic signals.

People were gathering around the bookies, making final bets. Some were wandering around in front of the stands, talking with friends or making new acquaintances. The women wore flowered dresses, and the men were comfortable in slacks and sports jackets. She watched the women, walking carefully in their high-heeled sandals over the uneven grass. It was a day to wear one's summer clothes one last time before the cold of winter froze to the marrow those who remained. Those who could afford it flew south with the birds, looking for warmer climes.

Suddenly, Mr. Grimes, the owner of the art gallery, stopped beside her. "Got a tip for you," he said out of the corner of his mouth. "You bought that painting; I owe you one. Next race, Blue Velvet. She's a cert," he muttered. Then he proclaimed loudly, "Nice day," and quickly walked away.

Alison smiled to herself. She had her hot tip and quickly found her favorite bookie, Wily Willie, and placed her bet with him.

"Good odds," he said, eying her keenly. "Know something I don't?"

She shrugged her shoulders. "It's all a gamble," she said. "You know that, Willie." Then as she turned to watch the horses being led around the paddock, she noticed a familiar figure. It was the vet, Harry Hastings, standing with his back to her. She recognized him by the shape of his head, his distinctive fair hair, and his sports jacket. He was talking seriously with one of the owners, and as soon as he saw her, he beckoned her over. Alison ducked under the railing and walked over to join them, and he introduced her to his clients, Dr. and Mrs. Nightingale.

"Harry says you bought a John Trentham," said Dr. Nightingale. "We have one too. You must come up to the house sometime and see it."

He looked so distinguished as he smiled gently at her. Alison smiled in return. She guessed from his measured tones that he was from London, and judging from his graying hair, she assumed he was in his early sixties; his wife perhaps was a little younger. Mrs. Nightingale looked as if she were from the hunting set, with her tweed jacket, matching pleated skirt, and sensible shoes.

"Come and visit us. I've read all your books," said Mrs. Nightingale, handing Alison a card that she produced from a jacket pocket. "We don't fox hunt anymore, but we still drag hunt. Come and hunt with us this year, and bring that old thoroughbred of yours."

"Thanks, I'd love to do that," said Alison. Her heart sang. Dr. Nightingale was not from London after all. He and his wife were locals; they had a John Trentham; and she had an invitation to visit them.

Alison wanted to ask the Nightingales about their John Trentham, but the jockeys were up, and the horses were leaving the paddock. "Wish us luck," they said, pointing at Blue Velvet.

So that's Blue Velvet, she thought. Nothing much to look at, and she doubted she would have bet on the horse without Mr. Grimes's encouragement. She and Harry walked over to the rail. She thanked him for the introduction and asked him if he were duty vet.

"Not today," he replied. "Today, I'm here to make my fortune."
She remembered the gossip that Harry's wife had left him for a wealthy businessman and taken the children with her. "Which one shall I choose?" he asked her. "How about College Boy?"

"The big chestnut? How about that little brown one, Blue Velvet, number 5."

"Is that your hot tip?" he asked her. "Are you sure? That's the Nightingales' horse. It's never won anything in its life."

A thought crossed Alison's mind about the reliability of Mr. Grimes's hot tip, but she said nothing. "Today could be the day," she said. "It's a tip hot enough to wager at least tea money on it."

"Win, show, or place?"

"According to my source, win, definitely."

He laughed and said, "Okay, if I win, I'll buy tea, and if I lose, you buy it. Which bookie did you use?"

Harry went to place his bet, and Alison went in search of the tearoom. It was full of people and noise, and most of the tables had dirty cups and plates. She found an empty table in front of the big window overlooking the racecourse and sat down. She could see the horses cantering down to the start and the jockeys standing in their stirrups. She hoped that Harry had managed to place his bet in time.

Alison noticed her reflection in the glass. Opening her purse, she took out her compact and quickly added a few touches of powder and a dab of lipstick—not enough that he would notice but just enough. She smiled, and the face in the mirror smiled back—blue eyes, fair hair, and strong chin. She had inherited the chin and the stubbornness that went with it from her father. She had a reputation for intuitiveness in her horse dealings that had earned her a degree of admiration. "Watch 'er; she knows her 'orses" was said behind her back. She was thinking about life and its uncertainties, about winning and losing, when Harry walked in and sat down opposite her.

"I bet all I had," he said, looking in her eyes. "How much did you bet?"

"I'll tell you after the race," she replied. She turned to look through her binoculars at the horses being loaded into the starting stalls. They had all gone in quietly and were waiting. The crowd below was waiting too.

As the gates opened, the announcer over the loudspeaker system called out, "They're off!" And the horses were away, galloping over the course, with dirt and grass flying and riders crouched low. The crowd let out a roar as a tired waitress came over to ask what they'd like to order.

"Two teas," said Harry. "And we'd like some sandwiches and biscuits."

"We're out of sandwiches and biscuits," she replied.

"Two teas, then, and cake, if you have any," said Harry. He looked intently through his binoculars at the horses that were rounding the turn and galloping down the straightaway toward the finish.

Both he and Alison were standing up now, part of a crowd that had gathered in front of the window. There was a murmur of excitement as the announcer said, "It's Alleycat in the lead, the Entertainer second, and Blue Velvet third. College Boy is still four lengths behind the front runners." The pitch of his voice rose in excitement as he continued, "They're at the eighth pole, and now it's Blue Velvet making her move. She's coming on fast on the outside." His voice sounded his surprise. "Now it's Blue Velvet in the lead and at the post. It's Blue Velvet first by half a length, over Alley Cat second, and in third place, the Entertainer."

There was a general murmur of discontent from the crowd; the favorite had lost again that day for the sixth time.

"Alison, how much did you bet?" Harry asked as they sat down.

"Two hundred pounds," she replied, blue eyes gleaming.

"I had no idea that I was having tea with a gambling woman. Let's celebrate with champagne. By the way, who gave you the tip?"

"I never reveal my sources," she laughed, looking at him from beneath her lashes. She thought he sounded very calm for a man whose hands were shaking as he held the binoculars. Her own heart was pounding so hard, she thought he would hear it.

"Would you like to meet Colossus?" she asked him. "He's still here."

"A horse called Colossus? Of course I want to meet him. Did you buy him already?"

"Well, maybe. It depends on you and the X-rays. Want to own part of a racehorse?"

As he sat opposite her, he found to his surprise that he couldn't stop looking at her. He was fascinated, and he didn't care who noticed. All he knew was that it had been a long, long time since he'd had so much fun with anyone. Alison noticed the intensity of his gaze and found herself equally absorbed in him. People in the vicinity, including the Pollocks and her housekeeper, Mrs. Crocket, noticed too, for it was a small town and everyone knew everyone else's business.

Two teas were placed on the table in front of them almost without their noticing it, along with two pieces of chocolate cake. They sipped the hot liquid, nibbled on the cake, and argued happily, as even winners will, about whether to see the new horse first, or to drink champagne, or to collect their winnings. Finally, Harry said, "How about we look at the horse and then have dinner and champagne at the Dog and Duck? I think I owe you one after today."

Alison agreed. Well satisfied, they finished their tea and looked out the window at the green grass of the race course and the green and brown fields beyond. They knew that the land gradually rose until the fields gave way to the moors, springy heather, and sheep.

Harry said, "Shall we go collect our winnings?" While he paid for the tea, Alison went to see William Wiggins, Esquire, the bookie.

The fact that Blue Velvet had seemed a foregone conclusion to a few had not been obvious to many, and consequently, Alison had won a tidy return on her investment: five thousand pounds.

William Wiggins, Esquire—Wily Willy to his friends—looked down his large nose at her, studying her carefully with his sharp brown eyes, taking in every detail and missing nothing, as he counted out her winnings. He wore a brown felt hat with a large white feather in it. His many-colored jacket was so wide at the shoulders and loose fitting that it seemed as if it wished to give the impression that its owner was larger than life.

"The lucky lady herself," he said. "Have a care going home. Would you like to risk a little on the next race?" he asked hopefully.

Alison smiled sweetly at him and said, "Not today, Willy." She and Harry then made their way to the far side of the racecourse where the horses were stabled.

"By the way, Harry, how much did you bet?" she asked.

"All I had, fair lady," he said, looking down at her with his clear, bright blue eyes. "All I had."

Colossus was waiting impatiently for them. A big, black strapping colt—that was how Harry described him—with a star on his forehead, his plain head was made more attractive by his large, dark intelligent eyes. He whinnied hopefully at Alison as she stood by the door of his stall.

"He wants me to take him home." she said. "Jimmy, could you bring him out for me?" she asked his groom. "I want to show him to Dr. Hastings, and we'll need the X-rays, too, please." Once outside the stall, she gave Colossus a carrot, which he crunched appreciatively. "Well, what do you think?" she asked Harry.

"Let's see him move," he said. As Colossus was walked up and down the breezeway, Harry whistled under his breath. He looked at the layback of Colossus shoulder, the amount of bone below the knee, the well-shaped feet, and the overreach of the hind hooves. "How do you find these horses?" he asked her.

"I don't; they find me. Isn't he beautiful?"

"Yes, but how much?"

"Not a lot. He was an expensive two-year-old that never fulfilled his potential. The owners were desperate. They'd tried everything, and they knew I could retrain him."

Harry had to admit to himself that Alison had a gift for finding amazing horses for sale at amazing prices. He looked closely at the X-rays, and then he looked at her with a new respect. "He's clean," he said.

"I love beautiful things, Harry," she said, stroking Colossus's neck. "Horses, dogs—I can pick them. I look at their movement. I look at their conformation and temperament. People, I'm not so good at." She didn't want to say men in particular, but she thought it.

Harry thought of the one encounter he'd had with Alison's husband and silently agreed with her assessment. Alison had introduced them at the Dog and Duck one lunchtime, and although Harry had been impressed by Jack's smile and outgoing personality at first, he'd seen something unexpectedly dark behind that smile. He hoped he was wrong.

"This horse wants to jump," she said. "He's a steal at the price. It was love at first sight."

"How do you know that he wants to jump?"

"He told me so."

"Oh, is that how you do it?" Harry said, looking at her quizzically. "I had been wondering,"

"Don't look at me like that," she said. "You're my friend, Harry Hastings. Between you and me, his pedigree says flat racing, long distance, on his sire's side, but his dam is from Ireland, and I know they did some jumping. Look at the way he's put together. He'll go three miles with no problems, but the sale is subject to the X-rays. If you say they're clean, the horse is mine."

Harry walked around the horse, picking up the feet, running his hands down the legs, and then opening the mouth and checking the teeth. Colossus stood quietly, his ears pricked, watching Alison.

"So what did he say exactly?" Harry teased.

"I'll never tell. I have my reputation you know," she laughed. "This is the way it went down. He won't run. When the gate opens, he stands there, so after the owners had tried everything, they dumped him."

He wondered at her humor and the risks that she took. "But how do you know he'll jump?"

"He told me so. Trust me, Harry; he'll jump." Alison always was happy around the horses. People thought she had a gift, but she knew it was all about being observant—and lucky. Tigger's behavior had taken her completely by surprise, but she blamed herself. She had missed the warning signs. There were always warning signs with horses—people, too—and if one missed them, it could be dangerous.

"No starting gate. Hm-m-m, maybe he will do it," Harry said thoughtfully.

"He will! He will! He told me so, didn't you, boy?" She patted Colossus gently on the neck before putting him away. "Better a life with me jumping than the alternative. You're much too beautiful for that. Come on, Harry," she said. "Colossus is coming home with me tonight, and I have to sign some papers, go home, and get the horse box. "Are you in or not?"

"I'm in," said Harry in the euphoria of the moment, and he laughed. Together, they stepped out into sunshine. He was glad that Jack was out of town. He found he was looking forward very much to their dinner together. "Blue Velvet is not the only racehorse the Nightingales own," he said. "They enjoy buying and selling one or two every year."

She wondered what they would make of Colossus.

He fixed his blue eyes on hers and looked at her with intensity. She found herself returning the gaze, a sudden flight of butterflies in her stomach.

"They are such lovely people, Alison. I'm glad I was able to introduce them to you. As well as being a real estate developer, he's been a local doctor for years. His wife used to write books similar to yours, and his family's been here for generations. Do give them a call."

Alison took out the card that Barbara Nightingale had given her and read, "Nightingale Properties—Sales and Investments," Her brow furrowed. "Do you think this is the right one?"

"Oh, yes. Their home phone number's on the back. See? I'm sure they'd love to show you around. They have an estate with acres and acres of land—horses too."

"Harry, did you invest in their building project next to the racecourse?"

"Me?" he laughed, shaking his head. "No. My brother John did, though. He's quite a go-getter and a big believer in Dr. Nightingale's ideas. They want to put Roystone on the map."

It was later, on the way home with Colossus, that she realized she had forgotten to ask Harry about the painting. It was then she gripped the steering wheel in dismay. If he knew Barbara's books were similar to hers, he had to have read her books too. First Mr. Grimes and Mr. Pollock, then probably the Reverend, and now Harry. They had all read her books—romances she had written for women, all published under a pen name. In London, it had been easy to retain her anonymity. What had never occurred to her was that in a small town like Roystone, where everyone knew everyone else's business, they would know hers as well as she knew theirs! She felt as if people she knew had looked into the depths of her soul. Then foolishly, on her last book, which had been such a success, at Beaky's insistence, she had included a small photograph of herself on the back cover. And then there were the articles in the local newspaper. *I am a silly little bird,* she thought. Of course everyone knew who she was. Of course everyone had read her books. Was she not a local celebrity? It was then another terrible thought struck her. *They all know my husband Jack is never home!* No wonder there were whispers in the off-license and in the Dog and Duck as well, no doubt. Her face went scarlet with embarrassment. And then her grip on the steering wheel relaxed. *Everyone knows who I am and yet how kind they are to me.* There was no need to worry. She had been accepted, books and all, into the community of this small town. She was well and truly home.

6

When Alison arrived home later with Colossus, she put him in a big indoor/outdoor loose box with plenty of shavings, hay, and water. She called Tigger and Captain in from the pasture, fed them, and put down more bedding in their loose boxes before returning to the house. By the time she walked in the door, it was already dusk, and she could hear the phone ringing in the kitchen. It was Harry.

"What time's dinner?" she asked him.

"Alison, I can't go tonight. I am so sorry. Please forgive me. Alan Dodson's wife is having a baby. He was duty vet, and he asked me to take emergencies for him, and old Fred Barnley's mare has colicked. He lives way on the other side of the valley, so it'll be late by the time I get finished." He hesitated briefly and then said sadly, "I've got more bad news. I spoke with my solicitor, John Stokes, and I can't buy into the horse, Alison. My divorce isn't final yet. For me, it's always money, you know."

Alison tried to hide her disappointment. "Don't worry, Harry. Another time," she said brightly. "You'll regret the horse, though."

"I know I will," he said mournfully. "And the dinner—I regret that already. I was looking forward to celebrating with you … I tell you what. If I get finished early, perhaps I could stop by your place on my way home. I have some more information on your painting. My aunt Beth, the rector's wife—I think you met her already—said she found some old newspaper clippings, and she wants you to have them."

Alison's heart leapt. "Come on by. I'll put the kettle on for you. I have some fancy tea I've been saving. See you when you get here."

Was it the thought of seeing Harry that made her feel so effervescent or the possibility of more information about the picture? Perhaps both. Whichever it was, she suddenly felt a wave of happiness.

And then, just as suddenly, Alison felt tired. It had been a long day. *Damn, damn, damn,* she thought. She had been looking forward to a dinner out and a celebration. Dutifully, she checked the answering machine to see if there were any messages from Jack and was glad when there were none.

The day's not over yet. I'm going to celebrate my win and my new horse, and I'm going to look for that fancy tea for Harry, she thought. She'd call Lisa and tell her all about everything in the morning. She found a bottle of her favorite champagne in the cellar and opened it, letting the cork hit the ceiling, enjoying the sight of the pink fizzy liquid filling her glass. She was hungry and was frying up some chicken and enjoying her second glass of champagne when there was a knock at the front door. She was surprised to see Johnny Pollock on the doorstep. His short brown hair was slicked down on top of his head, and she couldn't help thinking how much thinner and older he looked since last she saw him. *It must have been … two years ago at the Dog and Duck,* she thought. Until his mother had set her straight, she had assumed the rumors were true, that he had joined the navy to avoid marrying his pregnant girlfriend. Alison wondered why he had returned. She opened the door, saying, "What are you doing here, Johnny? I thought you were away at sea these days. Your mum said you'd joined the Royal Navy."

Johnny looked hopefully at Alison. "Well, that's what I'm here about, Mrs. Simons. I thought maybe you could help me, being as how I'm on the lam right now." Seeing her uncomprehending stare, he explained, "I left the navy a bit sudden, like."

Alison felt torn. She couldn't leave Fred and Moira Pollock's son standing on the doorstep, but her gut feelings told her to leave him outside. His reputation before joining the navy had not been a savory one. Mrs. Pollock had confided sadly to her late one evening, just before closing time at the Dog and Duck. "He had to go," she said. "Our only boy. He had gambling debts he couldn't pay. In the end, we took care of them, but we told him he had to join the navy and do something with himself. He didn't want the same kind of life we have here. We had such high hopes. Where did we go wrong?"

In the end, reluctantly and against her better judgment, Alison invited him into the kitchen.

"I hear that you had a successful day at the races," Johnny began when they were sitting down at the kitchen table.

She looked at him quickly. "Where did you hear that?" She saw him looking at the bottle of champagne and the glass, but she didn't offer him any. She intended to be in control of the situation.

"Oh, round about. It's a small town," he said carefully, his eyes refusing to meet hers. Then he said nervously, "I thought maybe you could lend me couple of thousand."

"A couple of thousand? I don't keep that kind of cash here, Johnny. How about your family?" It was then that she remembered that her winnings from the race were still in her purse. She had left it on the table in the entryway, meaning to put the money in the safe after dinner.

"No, Mom and Dad don't even know I'm here. I thought I'd try and get out of the country. Brenda and me, we want to go to Australia."

"With the military police on your tail? Not much hope of that. You should go back and work it out with the navy. It's never a good idea to run away. I tell you what. Promise me you'll go back to your ship, and I'll lend you two hundred pounds. You can pay me back later." She was unwilling to send him away with nothing. She knew that she had two hundred pounds in cash in the safe that was in the study. She'd give him that. She rose quickly and after walking into the study, she closed the door and opened the safe. She always kept a little cash at home for emergencies; this was an emergency. Johnny was still sitting at the table when she returned but suddenly she felt uneasy. Had he seen something? Had he followed her?

"Here's the money, Johnny. I think you'd better go now," Alison said.

He smiled his thanks, but she noticed that his eyes were suddenly hard and again, they could not meet hers. She opened the front door for him, and he slipped out into the night.

It was dark now, with no stars. An owl whoo-whooed close by, and she jumped. The air felt sharply cold and damp. There was a car in the driveway with its running lights on. Johnny Pollock had not come alone; someone was in the car waiting for him. She closed the door and locked it as tightly as she could.

Damn, she thought. *Maybe Jack was right. Maybe a security system would be a good idea. I should get the gate fixed too.*

Alison shivered but not from the cold that had crept in through the door as Johnny left. This was a nervous kind of shivering. Something in the kitchen was different … but what? She finished the chicken and a salad before deciding to soak in a hot bath while waiting for Harry.

The house was old—the stairs creaked as she climbed them, and the whitewashed walls were a little uneven. She remembered playing on the stairs as a child with her best friend, Lisa, sliding down the banisters and tiptoeing in and out of the bedrooms. They spent many happy hours looking for ghosts of long-dead Forsters, in and under the four-poster beds, but the four-poster beds and the chamber pots were now long gone. *How silly we were,* she thought.

The ceiling in her bedroom sloped down gradually to the window, and on the wall opposite the bed was her favorite painting that she had inherited from her father. It was the one she wanted Harry to see. She'd kept it in the living room for a while but had eventually moved it to the bedroom, because it made visitors uneasy. It was of a life-sized fox with a dead rabbit between its paws. The fox was sitting at the entrance to its den, looking with bared teeth at another fox, which was creeping out of the trees behind it. The frame was an old one, made of wood and painted in a soft gold tone.

Each time she looked at it, she felt there was always some new detail to admire that had previously escaped her attention. She enjoyed sitting by the open window, especially in summer, and thinking about what a treasure it was.

She ran a bath for herself and drank another glass of champagne, slowly savoring the idea of lying in the warm water. She turned off the taps and was walking into the linen cupboard to get a clean towel when the lights went off.

Alison stood there in darkness so thick that she couldn't see anything … but she heard the door click as it closed behind her. *What's happening? What's that strange smell?* It was then that the memory hit her like a blinding flash of light—a memory from childhood. She was standing in the fifth bedroom. She had found the door unlocked and crept in there. The room was empty but … something was in the closet— something wrapped in white cloth. She had stepped into the closet to see what it was, and somehow the door had swung closed behind her. Terrified and nauseated from the strange odor that the cloth emitted, she had screamed and fallen down in a dead faint. Fortunately, her grandfather had heard her scream and found her there moments later. As he picked her up and carried her out of the room, he said, "I told you to stay out of here. This room is not for children. Promise me, Alison. You must promise you will never go into that room again."

She promised him and, although curious, had kept her promise and never opened the door to the room again.

Now, her heart pounding, Alison fought the memory and felt her way to the door. She took a deep breath, steadied herself, and opened the door. The rest of the house was in darkness too. She moved slowly across the hall, found the phone in her bedroom, and lifted the receiver. There was no dial tone. *Don't worry*, she told herself. *Your cell phone is downstairs in your purse on the table.* She could easily get it, and there were plenty of flashlights in the kitchen. *Probably just a blown fuse*, she reassured herself.

She looked through the bedroom window. She could see nothing outside, for the sky was overcast, covering any light from the moon or stars. Before she could feel her way to the stairs, she heard voices—and they were coming from inside the house. Her heart began to pound again. Where was Harry? She really needed him now.

She crept to the top of the stairs, tiptoed down halfway, and peered over the banister. She could see flashes of light coming from the study. The sound of men's low voices again reached her in the silence. The blackness was so thick that it closed around her nose and mouth and almost choked her.

"It's bolted to the floor," she heard one man say.

"I'll soon get her to give us the combination."

They're trying to open the safe! she thought. Where had she heard that voice before? Her heart gave a lurch. Wasn't it Ben Jones?

"Don't hurt her," another one said, and she recognized Johnny Pollock's loud whisper. "I didn't agree to that."

She knew they would be coming to get her, and she panicked until she remembered something—her father's old shotgun. It was an antique, but it still worked. She used it sometimes to kill rats and other vermin. It was in the bottom drawer of the chest in her bedroom.

Now that her eyes had adjusted to the darkness, she could see the pinpoints of light. The intruders were walking out of the study—there were three of them. There was no more time for thinking; she must act quickly. She turned quickly to go back up the stairs, and as she did so, the old stairs creaked and betrayed her. Immediately, their flashlights were on her. She ran to the bedroom and tried to close and lock the door, but they were up the stairs and through the door in an instant. One of them grabbed her and threw her backwards on the bed. The light from the three flashlights blinded her.

"All we want, Mrs. Simons, is the combination to the safe. We want the money you won today."

"Johnny, is that you? I can't believe you're doing this."

"Believe it." A heavy hand slapped her roughly three times across the face, while strong arms held her arms over her head.

She gasped for breath and opened her mouth, trying to scream, but she was so dazed and afraid that no sound came out.

"Now, Mrs. Simons, the combination to the safe. We want the money."

She managed to make a strange, guttural, howling sound. "Let me go!" She struggled to escape, but it was no use. They were too powerful for her. She felt someone's hand covering her mouth, half suffocating her. She lay quietly, trying to breathe.

"Now, give me the combination to the safe." It was the same voice; the same question, raw and insistent. She was overwhelmed by their smell, their closeness, and the pressure of their hands on her arms holding her down. She retched and tried to scream at the same time, in sheer terror at the confinement of her body. There was a terrible pressure on her chest. Someone was kneeling on her. She couldn't breathe! The hand over her mouth was removed.

"There's ... no money in the safe," she managed to whisper.

"Where is it?"

"In my handbag on the hall table." She heard the sound of footsteps running down the stairs.

"I got it!" That was Johnny's voice. "Come on, Mike. We got it. Let's get out of here!"

"I should finish you off," her captor snarled. "No witnesses." The pressure on her neck and throat increased. This voice, she did not know.

Suddenly, in the silence, she heard the sound of a car pulling up on the gravel in front of the house. She fought to retain consciousness. She heard a car door slamming and a voice shouting, "Alison! Alison, are you okay?"

"Help," she managed to call out before the hand closed across her mouth again. This time she bit down as hard as she could. The man howled with pain.

"You bitch," she heard him say as the hand covering her mouth and the pressure on her chest were removed. "Help! Help!" she shouted again, able to breathe at last.

She could hear sounds of a scuffle at the front door and then a thundering up the stairs … and then all hell broke loose.

"Go get 'em, girls!" That was Harry's voice, and into the room burst three large black shapes—the dogs. Harry carried a large flashlight in one hand and a large stick in the other.

The dogs were barking; Harry was shouting. "Alison, are you all right? What's going on here?"

This was more than the intruder had bargained for. He escaped, almost knocking Harry over as he tumbled himself down the stairs and out of the front door, the dogs at his heels.

"Alison, are you all right? Are you hurt?" Harry shone the flashlight over her, over the room, and even under the bed.

She sat up, gasping, choking, and coughing, trying to catch her breath. Harry took her in his arms and held her, feeling her heart pounding and feeling her arms tighten around him. "When I called, the phone didn't ring, and I got worried. I knew Jack was out of town and that something was wrong. If you can tell me where the fuse box is, we can get some light."

"Downstairs in the kitchen by the door," she managed to get out. "Just don't leave me, Harry. It's so dark; I don't want to be alone."

"Come with me, then." He helped her to stand up and dragged a blanket off the bed to put around her shoulders. With his arm around her, they felt their way slowly down the stairs and into the kitchen. He found the fuse box and turned on the switches, flooding the house in light.

Alison blinked in the sudden brightness but she could see the concern on Harry's face, along with two large black dogs. She collapsed onto a kitchen chair and put her head in her hands. "Harry," she said, "you saved my life again."

Alison could tell her face was swollen and bruised. She knew from the grim expression on Harry's face, his mouth set in a thin line, how great was his level of concern. They both knew he had arrived just in time. He turned away and busied himself with putting water into the kettle and lighting the gas stove.

"This is all my fault," he whispered. "If I had been here earlier, this wouldn't have happened. Too many people knew about the money you won."

"Harry," she said again, "thank goodness you arrived when you did. They wanted the combination to the safe. They didn't realize the money was still in my handbag."

"Still in your handbag?" he repeated.

"Oh, they got the money. I gave them that. You know what's in the safe, Harry? My laptop, two pages of research for my new book, and my dad's will." She laughed shakily. "You know, I was so scared my mind went a complete blank. I couldn't remember the combination. Maybe I should write it down somewhere."

He looked at her. "Maybe you should." He poured hot water into the teapot but then hesitated, asking, "Got anything a little stronger we could pour in the tea?" Alison waved distractedly in the direction of the cupboards and he began to look, opening and closing doors swiftly until he found a half a bottle of brandy. He added some to the cups of tea. Alison grasped the cup with both hands and drank greedily.

Suddenly, car headlights illuminated the kitchen window. Soon after, there was a hammering on the front door and a voice called out, "Are you all right, luv?"

Harry quickly answered the door, and Alison thought that one of the men standing outside, a man of considerable size, could easily have broken down the door if Harry had delayed opening it.

"Can we come in?" the smaller man asked. "I'm Sergeant Standing, Jennifer's dad. This is Constable Combs." From the doorway, the sergeant took in all the details—Alison's distressed appearance, her bruised face, the blanket wrapped around her. "As soon as the call came in, we were on our way. Jennifer thinks the world of you, you know. You're our famous author, Mrs. Simons. Couldn't have anything happen to you now, could we?"

Alison gulped, overwhelmed, and could say nothing.

"Good evening, Dr. Hastings," said the constable. "We caught two men running down the driveway, and we found this envelope, full of money on one of them. What's been goin' on here?"

Alison explained what had happened. "Three men broke in and turned off the electricity. At least two of them attacked me. They wanted the combination to the safe, and they wanted the money I won at the races. I recognized two of the voices but not the third. After I told them where the money was, one of them tried to strangle me." Alison broke into sobs at the thought that someone would try to kill her. "No witnesses, he said."

Harry longed to comfort her, but instead he told his side of the story, "I had an emergency call, but I'd promised Alison I would stop by on my way home. As I was crossing the valley, I could see the house with all the lights on—and then suddenly, her house was in darkness. I called her on my mobile, but the phone didn't ring. That was when I called the police. I knew something was wrong."

"Your husband out of town, again, Mrs. Simons?" asked the sergeant, looking carefully at Harry.

"Yes," Alison answered quietly.

"Do you usually keep your kitchen window like this?" asked the constable, indicating the window that was wide open.

"No, no," said Alison. *I knew something was different after Johnny Pollock left*, she thought. *It was the window.* "Johnny Pollock must have opened it. He came by earlier and asked me to lend him some money. That's how they got in."

"Big windows look good," said the sergeant, "but they give easy access. You need to put in a security system of some kind. I'm surprised your husband hasn't put one in already."

The two policemen looked at the safe, still locked. They looked at her bedroom, and then they examined all the other rooms in the house to make sure there was no one hiding anywhere. Finally, they walked around the outside of the house and then checked the stable.

Constable Combs came back into the house asked Alison to identify the two men they had caught running down the driveway. Alison followed him outside, with Harry and the dogs close behind her. She peered into the back of the police car. It was Johnny Pollock and someone she did not know—a small, dark, stocky man, perhaps someone Johnny knew from the navy. He was nursing his hand. He was the one who had made the marks on her throat. He was the one who had tried to kill her!

"We found a third man hiding in a ditch," the constable said. "Can you identify this man? Was this one of the men who broke into your home and attacked you?" It was the Welshman Ben Jones! He was shame-faced and refused to look at her. She clutched her blanket around her more securely and held onto Harry's arm. She looked at all three with horror and disgust. *What did I ever do to them? How could they? How could they? For revenge? Money? For kicks?* She thought she had heard Ben's voice earlier in the darkness. She remembered inviting him into the house when she had purchased the mare from him several years ago. He would have had plenty of time to walk into the study and see the safe. She began to shiver violently.

"I think that's all Alison can tell you tonight," said Harry, putting his arm around her protectively.

"Sorry, but we need a statement tonight, Mrs. Simons, and you must see the medical examiner immediately," said the sergeant. "I've put in a call for a woman constable. She'll drive you to the hospital. We're radioing ahead now, and she'll bring you home. Mr. Simons is where? Can we contact him?"

"Jack's in New York," said Alison. "I'm not sure where, exactly. He's putting in a security system for a big company over there. Very hush-hush. I ... I'm not sure when he'll be back. He said he'd call. I ... I can give you his card and a new phone number."

"Thank you. Dr. Hastings, we need a statement from you now, sir, either here or at the station."

"I'll make it here," said Harry. "I'll wait here for you, Alison, and make sure everything's safe."

"Constable Standing will take your statement then, sir," said the sergeant.

Alison whispered to Harry, "You were so right about Ben Jones. He did have a grudge against me. I didn't realize ..." She was shaken to the core that Jones felt so much anger against her.

It was a long night. The medical examiner turned out to be Dr. Nightingale. He examined Alison's throat at the hospital and took photographs of the bruising on her face and neck. Alison was glad it was someone that she knew, but his sympathy was too much for her. She kept dissolving into tears. She made a statement and signed it before being taken home by the woman constable. Harry and the dogs met the police car in the driveway, and he walked her into the house with his arm around her. There in the kitchen was his aunt, the rector's wife, Beth Durham.

"Alison," Mrs. Durham said, "I hope you don't mind my being here."

"I am so happy to see you, Mrs. Durham," said Alison. "How kind of you to be here."

"Call me Beth," she said. "We're so sorry this happened to you. Now, you must tell us if there's anything we can do to help."

Alison gave them both a smile of great gratitude. In truth, she was so tired she could hardly stand. The stairs to her bedroom looked like they were a mile high.

Harry said, "I'll sleep down here in the big armchair. The dogs will stay too."

"Harry," said Alison. "I am so tired—too tired to think what to say. I'm just so grateful to you both. There are lovely beds in the guestrooms. Please, wherever you want to sleep. I just don't want to be alone. Something ... something else happened tonight. I ... I think there's a ghost in the linen cupboard at the top of the stairs. It only appears when the lights go out, and it closes the door. Help yourselves to whatever you want. Please just leave the lights on. I don't want to be in the dark."

Beth helped her up the stairs. "Shall I run you a bath, Alison?"

"Too tired. I just took the sleeping pill the doctor gave me," Alison muttered and fell onto her bed, fully clothed. Beth pulled the blankets over her and then joined Harry downstairs.

Alison relaxed. *I'm safe*, she told herself. *Harry's here. Beth is here. The dogs ...* She was asleep in under a minute.

"Ghosts in the linen cupboard?" whispered Beth to Harry.

"Let's go and see," said Harry, but although they looked and looked, there was nothing. They even turned out the lights, but nothing happened. "Smells funny in here," he said. "Alison should take up the carpets and look for damp. What do you think?"

Beth shrugged. She, being of a practical nature, had noticed nothing. All she could see were shelves full of towels and sheets. Feeling silly but relieved, they walked downstairs. "There's nothing here," Beth said.

"I'm sure Alison's pretty level-headed," said Harry. "If she says she saw a ghost, something happened. Remember the old stories about this house? There's no smoke without fire."

When Alison awoke, it was broad daylight. She could hear birds chirping outside the bedroom window and the sound of the radio downstairs. Someone was in the kitchen. Mrs. Crocket? There was a cup of tea next to the bed that tasted wonderful. Slowly, she crawled out of bed and showered and dressed. She examined her face and neck in the bathroom mirror. Her face looked swollen, and the marks on her neck stood out in red. She definitely was going to have two black eyes in addition to the bruises on her neck. She remembered Harry and Beth and made her way, hobbling slowly and stiffly, down the stairs to look for them.

Mrs. Crocket was waiting for her, and she folded Alison in her arms and held her close. "You poor child. I'm so sorry I couldn't be here for you last night. Dr. Hastings told me all about what happened. I cooked him a big breakfast, but Mrs. Durham said she'd wait until she got home. Can you manage anything? I have to go soon, but I won't leave until I've cooked you something. I have to stop by the hospital again and see my sister. She's so poorly still."

Alison hugged her back. "Thank you for being here, Mrs. Crocket. I do hope your sister's getting better. Aagh, my face is so sore." Mentally, she struggled to keep up with Mrs. Crocket's cheerful voice.

"I'll be making you some ham and eggs, dear. Is that all right? Dr. Hastings left you an envelope on the table and a note." Alison sat down at the table, and Mrs. Crocket went on, "Here's another cup of tea. Oh, your face looks so swollen. My sister's got pneumonia this time, and she can't seem to get over it. We're worried about her, I can tell you. I can come back this evening, though, if you need me. I had to make sure you was feeling all right before I took off. Dr. Hastings took care of the horses for you, him and my husband.

How kind of them. Harry thought of everything, Alison thought.

Mrs. Crocket chattered on as she flipped the eggs over, "Ben Jones always had a nasty mean streak, but Fred Pollock's boy? What is the world coming to? His mom and dad must be so disappointed in him. They phoned this morning, and I answered it, because I didn't want it to go on ringing and wake you up. They are so sorry for all the trouble he's caused you. Oh, by the way, the telephone company came by too, very early, and mended the phone line for you. They heard it was out. Seems like they are all big fans of your books. They said they was all real worried about you. Jennifer Standing from the newspaper phoned too. She wants to know if she could she have another interview, and she said thanks to you, her horse is doing a lot better."

Alison hoped no one else would call for a while. She wanted to sit and be very, very quiet. Then she thought, *What lovely people they all are. I'd be glad to talk to them—later, maybe. There is always tomorrow or the day after.*

"Mrs. Durham can come by this afternoon for a while if you'd like her to," Mrs. Crocket said, "just to keep you company. And your neighbor from across the road, Mrs. Allan, stopped by asking if she could help. She heard the police cars last night and was worried about you."

How kind everyone is. How very kind, Alison thought. Then she realized that everyone was probably curious too, and the news would be all over town by now. Exciting news traveled the fastest. *What must everyone be thinking? Perhaps they're gathering in the off-license or the Dog and Duck at this very moment to discuss it.* She admitted to herself that she would have to put in the security system that Jack wanted and hoped he had finished designing it before he left town. She'd call his company first thing Monday morning and start the project.

As Alison sat and drank another cup of tea, she felt as if her head were encased in fluffy clouds, floating free, detached from the world. Mrs. Crocket put a plate of ham, eggs, and homemade bread and jam on the table in front of her, saying, "I've got to go see my sister, Mrs. S., but I'll look in on you later to make sure you're all right."

"You're a dear, Mrs. Crocket," Alison said. "I don't know what I'd do without you." She choked up with emotion but managed to say, "Please tell your sister to get well soon, and let me know if there's anything I can do for you and Mr. Crocket."

After Mrs. Crocket left, Alison took a deep breath. Everything on the plate in front of her smelled so good. Without thinking about it, she ate it all and downed another cup of strong tea. As she ate, she eyed the note and the large brown envelope in the middle of the table.

The note read, "I left you a present in the barn. She's called Lady." The large brown envelope had "For Alison" written on the outside.

Sitting in the kitchen alone, memories of everything she had experienced the previous evening began to overwhelm her. Alison pushed her chair back quickly and headed for the stable—being with the horses would be a calming experience. The three horses looked very happy. They obviously had been fed and their stalls mucked out. Captain had unlocked the gates between him and Tigger, and there they were, looking at her, their heads together, one gray and one brown. "You're good friends already," she said and gave each of them a piece of carrot before turning them both out on the pasture to play. She was very grateful to Harry and Mr. Crocket for taking care of them for her, as she was not feeling particularly strong that morning. She petted Colossus and gave him an extra carrot, and then she remembered the gift.

She looked in two of the spare loose boxes, but they were empty. In the third was a black-and-white dog—a border collie, her gift from Harry! The dog watched her intently as she stood by the open door, waiting for it to come to her. She didn't have to wait but a moment, for it was love at first sight. "Oh, you darling," she said, her face wet with her tears and the dog's kisses. What a good friend Harry was. Then Alison remembered the large envelope on the table. She walked back to the house, with the dog running and jumping beside her. She found a large bowl and filled it with water for Lady, left a message for Mrs. Crocket on her mobile to please bring some dog food with her when she returned, and then she sat down at the kitchen table.

It was time to open the large brown envelope. There was another note from Harry inside: "Forgot to mention this last night." Attached to the note were fragile and yellowed newspaper clippings. dated 1851. She unfolded them and read all about her house and when it was built and about John Trentham and his fiancée, Elsie Hastings. Another page, dated two months later, was devoted to the news of Elsie Hastings's marriage to a James Forster; nine months later, there was a birth notice, James Forster Jr. had been born to James and Elsie Forster. *So a Hastings had married a Forster all those years ago,* Alison thought. *Beth's facts were correct. What a fascinating story. Which man had Elsie Hastings loved? Was John Trentham her true love or James Forster?*

Alison suddenly realized she and Harry were related. They were not unalike in appearance. They both had fair hair, blue eyes, and strong chins, and both found a kinship with animals. Why hadn't she thought of it before?

Also included in the package was a book, recently published, called *The Meadstead Lands,* written by a Robert Hastings, whom she assumed was a relative of Harry's. It looked so interesting that she sat down in her favorite chair next to the fire in the living room to read it, but the print was so small that in spite of her best intentions, she fell asleep.

Over at the Dog and Duck, Mrs. Crocket listened to the message Alison left on her phone and for the first time that day, she smiled. She told Mrs. Pollock over lunch—as well as everyone else within earshot, "Dr. Hastings has given her a dog. It's just the ticket, just what Mrs. Simons needs. It'll keep her company. More's the pity, her husband doesn't. I'll have another shandy, if you please, Mr. P. A large one. I'm feeling really thirsty, and in view of what I just heard, it's a bit of a celebration."

Mrs. Pollock agreed with her, as did everyone else. "He's not much of a husband," she said. "I'll bet he hasn't come home yet neither."

Alison awoke with a start and found the little black-and-white dog sitting at her feet, watching her intently. She found an old blanket and laid it in a corner of the kitchen for the dog, but Lady ignored the blanket and remained glued to Alison's side. "Come on, Lady," she said. "Let's go for a walk before it gets any later. I'll show you around."

She walked down the gravel driveway to the open gate and then they followed the stone wall as it led them around the property. *Did last night really happen?* Alison asked herself. Out here in the daylight and the sunshine, it seemed unreal—until the cold wind made her face tingle, and then she remembered the sudden darkness, the violence, and the anger; it really had happened to her. That Ben Jones held a grudge against her was one thing, but to want to be avenged in such a way was beyond her comprehension. After all, they were both in the business of buying and selling horses, and what went around, came around. He might have purchased the next horse she sold, and it might have turned out to be the champion he felt he deserved. But she realized Ben Jones's anger toward her was another expression of his anger toward life. He had a feeling of being cheated out of something that was owed him. Was it her success with the horses or the fact that she was a woman that trampled the most on his ego? Or was it, perhaps, that she owned the house and twenty-five acres on the top of the hill, and he was only a tenant, renting his property? Who could tell? She, who prided herself on being a keen observer, had missed the warnings signs from him. She felt lucky to be alive.

She fed the horses their dinner, and when she arrived back at the house, Mrs. Crocket had been and gone, but there was a large bag of dog food waiting inside the front door and a note on the table: "Harry called. He says please call him back." There were several messages on the answering machine: one from her publisher, Beaky, that she ignored; one from Jennifer Standing of the *Roystone Herald*, begging her for another interview; and one from her best friend, Lisa. Last was a message from Jack: "Are you all right? The police said something about a burglary and an assault. Can't get home right now. I'm in the middle of something big—really big. I'll be home as soon as I can."

She returned Jack's call immediately, but the phone just rang and rang. She was glad the police had managed to contact him, but why couldn't she? She wondered about the "something big." She wondered about this trip to New York. She wondered why he was never ever there when she called him.

Next, she called Harry and left a message: "Thanks for Lady. She's beautiful. Please call me."

Then she returned Lisa's telephone call and was happy to hear her cheerful voice.

"Lisa," Alison said, "I bought a racehorse. I think he'll make a steeplechaser, and I need a trainer."

"You did? Lucky you. And I know a trainer near York. When can I come over and see him? Would Friday be too soon?"

"Friday's perfect. Did you hear about Harry Hastings rescuing me twice?"

"Twice. Lucky you. He's a doll."

"Oh, and I bought a Welsh pony, a three-year-old, as well."

"Alison, are you thinking of driving him? If you are, I'll bring a training cart. I've got one you can borrow."

After an hour on the phone, and some tears as Alison recounted all the events of the past week, she felt a lot steadier. She found that her friend's down-to-earth common sense always gave her a feeling of strength, and she valued their friendship. Lisa was an excellent trainer who rode and drove horses with a touch and insight that was magical to watch.

Then Alison phoned Mr. O'Reilly, the trainer near York. "My friend Lisa T. Jones recommended you," she said and went on to explain the problem with the starting gate. "Would you be willing to take Colossus and see if he has any jumping talent? He's almost four and a natural jumper."

"Mrs. Simons, we'd be glad to take him, but there are no guarantees that he will enjoy jumping now. Has he been gelded already? Geldings are so much easier to train for steeplechasing."

When Alison said that he had, the well-modulated but very cool voice went on to explain the fees for board and training, to which Alison agreed.

"Now, Mrs. Simons, what makes you think we can turn him into a jump horse?"

"Well," she replied, "the pedigree, you know," and she mentioned the sire and a few names from the dam's side.

At this, Mr. O'Reilly expressed more interest. "We'll definitely find out for you, Mrs. Simons. As a matter of fact, I have a couple of three-year-olds with similar pedigrees in a field waiting to be started. You may be on to something with your horse. Let's find out. The van will pick up him up next week. I'll fax you over a contract to sign. You can fax me a copy of all the papers you have on him, and I look forward to meeting you both."

Alison heaved a sigh of relief. *So far, so good.* She called her publisher, Beaky, and assured him she was working on the new novel, that no one had seen it, and that it was safe in the safe. She didn't tell him that so far, it consisted of only two pages of notes and a book called *The Meadstead Lands*, but it was a beginning.

8

Early on Friday morning, Alison saw Lisa's black SUV driving past the kitchen window hauling a trailer, and she and Lady ran to the barn to meet her.

"Alison, I brought you the training cart," Lisa called out. "And I'll leave it with you. I'm not using it right now. It'll be heavy enough for him to know he's pulling something but not heavy enough to scare him." She looked at her friend's bruised face and hugged her very gently. "Oh, Alison," she said, "you poor thing. What is wrong with this world? Ben Jones was absolutely wicked to do this to you. He's a monster, and he'll never get any more business from me or anyone else. I'll make sure of that."

Together, they ooohed and aaahed over Colossus. "Another great find, and where did you get that cute dog?" Lisa asked as Lady checked her out carefully. "I know. He's from Harry … with love?"

"Don't be silly," said Alison, trying to hide a smile. "Harry's a friend, that's all. I didn't get the chance to tell him the whole story on Colossus. One of the board of directors of the racecourse called me. A friend of his owned a young horse that didn't want to run and refused to break from the starting stall. Then, one day it refused to go anywhere near the starting stall, unseated the jockey, jumped the outside rail, and made its way back to the stable. Apparently, that was when they thought of me. They were thinking of a show jumper, but I took one look, and the word steeplechaser came into my mind. Anyway, the trainer you recommended is sending a van to collect him next week. Lisa, if Colossus has any jumping ability, perhaps if he wins his first race, I'll have a proposition for you, but … let's see what he thinks of being a steeplechaser first. Harry turned me down already, probably very wisely."

"What's the proposition?" Lisa asked.

Alison smiled "I'll tell you later, after that first race," she said. She was remembering all the times as teenagers they had bought and sold horses together. She purchased them, Lisa trained them, and together they sold them. They never lost any money. She thanked her lucky stars over and over for her grandmother who, in the long summer holidays, had passed on all her knowledge about horses to her. "What do you see, child? Don't just look for the pretty," her granny would say. "Look underneath the skin. Find the soul. If you can, use your sense of touch. And always listen. What is the horse saying to you? If you listen, he will tell you everything." Lisa was convinced the horses actually spoke to Alison, but Alison denied it. "Not in the way you think," she always said. "But they do tell me things." They had gone to many auctions together, and Alison had always been able to find them a special horse.

Now, Lisa appraised her friend. "You're looking far too thin and pale," she said. "Where's that husband of yours? He's never home to take care of you." Before Alison could respond, Lisa said with her usual directness, "As for Harry Hastings, even if he turned down your proposition, he's a good man with old-fashioned values. He cares more about the animals he takes care of than making a lot of money and owning a big house."

"As I said, he's wise man and a good man," Alison responded, her head down, busying herself with Tigger's harness. Her feelings for Harry were much too new and raw to share with anyone, even Lisa.

They longed Tigger in circles, hooking the long lines to his bridle and running them through the circle, making sure he was listening to them and bending his body in both directions before putting a harness on him. He was so willing that they attached the traces to the breaking cart and let him pull it. Lisa was very impressed with his progress. "We all miss old man Johnson," she said regretfully. "He had some lovely Welsh ponies. Tigger's been well started, and he has a wonderful mind. He'll soon trust you and forget whatever Ben did to him."

They walked back to the SUV, and Lisa unhooked the trailer. "Come on. Let's go out to lunch," she said.

"People will see me," Alison replied nervously. "I'm not ready."

"Yes, but with that hat and dark glasses, no one will recognize you," Lisa said quickly. "Come on; it'll be fun."

As Alison was hesitating, three cars raced up the driveway toward them and stopped abruptly. Pouring out of their vehicles with cameras and microphones on long booms were reporters from the local newspapers and the local television station—and Alison thought she recognized the call letters of a national television station too. *Was that Jennifer Standing's boyfriend?* she wondered. There were so many of them, she was overwhelmed. "What are you all doing here?" Alison asked them.

"Your publisher invited us. I'm Dale Sharp, from Independent Television," one of them said. "Didn't he tell you? He wants as much coverage of what happened to you as possible. He says you owe it to your fans. After all, you are a well-known writer, Mrs. Simons, and you do have a lot of readers."

Mentally hanging Beaky, Alison smiled somewhat grimly at the image of watching him swing at the end of a rope. "Okay, then, just a few questions," she said, wondering why they all looked seedy. "We were just leaving."

The reporters gathered around Alison, bombarding her with questions, their cameras a sea of flashing lights.

"Where's your husband, Mrs. Simons? Still out of town?"

"Did you know your attackers?"

"Do you think Dr. Hastings saved your life?"

"How close are you and Dr. Hastings? Good friends or something more?"

The questions came at Alison too quickly for her to answer, and she could feel herself fading—tears weren't far away. They were crowding her, physically and mentally. It was all too much, too soon, and it reminded her somehow of the assault upon her, of being held down.

A young man armed with a movie camera spoke up next. "How about some pictures without the hat and glasses?" He looked a lot like Jennifer Standing's young man.

Alison shook her head weakly. *Are they wolves, moving in for the kill?* She had been backing up steadily and was now leaning against the car for support.

"That's enough for today, everyone," Lisa said forcefully to the reporters. "I'm sure there'll be champagne for all when Alison's next book is published" She elbowed her way through the crowd, opened the passenger door of the car, and pushed Alison and the dog inside.

"And I'm sure my publisher will let you know when that will be," Alison promised them through the open window.

Lisa got in the car and started the engine in a flash. "Okay if I drive over the grass?" she asked.

"Oh yes, Lisa, get going. If they get in the way, drive over them too. Let's go to the Three Brothers Café. We can easily outrun them in this," said Alison wildly. "Believe me, I know all the shortcuts to the Three Brothers Café. I'll feel better after a big lunch. I'm hungry, that's all." She began to laugh a little hysterically. "What a morning."

"It has been a little over the top," replied Lisa reassuringly. "But a good meal at the Three Brothers Café will set us both to rights. Fasten your seatbelt and hang on to your hat! Here we go." And the big car accelerated down the driveway.

As Alison predicted they easily left their pursuers far behind and found a parking space on a secluded street not far from the café. "Come on, Alison," said Lisa. "Let's make a run for it." They made a quick dash for the café and on arrival, with no sign of the press, they breathlessly pushed open the heavy wooden door. Once inside the café, they walked slowly up the narrow wooden stairs, inhaling the aromas. They could hear the sound of people talking and eating as they approached the dining room. Alison spied an empty table overlooking the street below. This was her favorite table, next to the window, with a bird's-eye view of the world and the people in it. Alison felt her luck was finally changing.

"Lisa, I'm so sorry about all those reporters. Beaky is such a rat. He's always conjuring up publicity stunts to get my name in the news. I just wish he'd let me know in advance. He never does. Oh, I take that back. Come to think of it, he left a couple of messages on my phone that I forgot to listen to. He always says, 'Now Alison, people need to remember who you are!' Anyway, it's done now. What shall we eat? I'm hungry. Eggs and sausages and tomatoes and toast and coffee."

"Me, too," Lisa replied. "Maybe even some mushrooms."

The waiter approached the table and greeted Alison warmly. "Mrs. Simons, how nice to see you here."

"So much for the disguise," said Alison to Lisa. They placed their orders and then she said, "Well, what do you think? Will Tigger pull that cart?"

"Born for it, my dear. Tigger is born for it. You've done it again. He'll mature out at about thirteen-two, and look at the bone he has. He'll be plenty powerful for you to drive but not too big. You could even ride him. You'll have a lot of fun with that pony, driving around your own property, and then they hold meets and shows outside of York. You'll be able to go up there too. There's lots of driving around here. You just never noticed it. Did you see the way he extends at the trot? Unbelievable. How much did you pay for him? I'll double it."

Alison smiled. "Well, if my financial situation doesn't improve I may have to sell him," she said. "But I've always wanted a good driving pony. Looks like I've found one."

"You are so lucky."

"Lucky with horses; unlucky in love," Alison replied sadly.

"Hey, lots of us don't have either." Lisa laughed ruefully, shaking her head until her long earrings jangled. "My ex is suing me for alimony."

"Which ex is that?" Alison asked.

They both laughed, and Alison began to relax. She enjoyed Lisa's company. Lisa, with her black hair and flashing dark eyes, was so different from Alison, but she was such a strong, capable, passionate woman that Alison always felt secure with her. Life felt almost normal again. "And your boys?" she questioned her. "How are they?"

"Growing," answered Lisa. "They're like colts, always growing. And their feet. You should see their feet. You are so lucky to have your Welsh pony. His feet won't get much bigger, and he'll never need shoes."

Again, they both laughed, but before Alison had a chance to reply, without warning, a stream of well-wishers began to visit them at the table. The Nightingales again invited Alison for a tour of their home. "Do come by any time."

Mr. Grimes stopped by the table to ask how she was enjoying *Gone Away*. "I'll call you right away if I can find another John Trentham."

The rector stopped by and wished her well. "Will you be in church on Sunday?" he inquired.

She felt so welcome; there was so much kindness that Alison was close to tears again. Home. How lovely it was to feel she was home. It gave her heart a lovely warm feeling. The only jarring note was when she asked Dr. Nightingale about the new shopping center.

"All life is change, my dear," he said. "The town needs the money. Many local people have invested with me in this enterprise. We must move forward. The racing is popular, and the town needs to benefit from it. All of us need to benefit, not just the racing fraternity. Think of the employment, the new jobs for the builders—the hotels, the banquet facility, the exhibition hall, and a place, finally, to park the buses."

Alison hadn't thought of it from that point of view. It made her feel that she was being selfish, and yet … "But Dr. Nightingale, is this the best time for this kind of investment? The town council built a market on the old bus station site, and it went bankrupt."

"Yes, yes, my dear," he said soothingly. "I admit mistakes have been made, but it's all location, location, and timing. This one is perfect, and it's on some land that my family has owned for generations. There'll be room for a new bus station and a new conference center. The busses will no longer have to park on the streets, and the Saturday market will be held there, too. So convenient for everyone."

"But the town … its uniqueness, its …" Words failed her. How could she describe how she felt? "It'll just be wall-to-wall cars, like all the other towns." It was all she could think of to say, but her dismay was evident in her voice.

"Progress, my dear; we must move forward." He was smiling at her, but his eyes told her he had made up his mind.

She would ask Harry what he thought. Surely everyone didn't want the town to "move forward" and yet, in a way, Dr. Nightingale was right. It would provide the employment that was so desperately needed.

She sighed. She felt out of step with the world. She longed for peace and quiet, but the town longed for busyness. She longed for a sense of community and harmony; it longed for bigger buildings and more money. Too many towns where she had stayed felt like the muddled center of a rose that had developed too quickly, becoming full blown with no identity, when it should have been a bud. Even though Roystone had been a small town for centuries, would it lose its character and become a town where no one knew anyone, not even their neighbors, and worse, no one cared?

After lunch, Lisa drove Alison home, keeping a wary eye open for the press. Alison fed Lady the sausage she had saved for her—extra special for being a good girl.

"What a meal—it should last me for a week," said Lisa. "I need a long walk."

Alison looked at her friend and nodded her agreement. "Me too," she replied. "Well, usually I would, but today my legs still feel a bit weak. Silly, isn't it?" But she knew Lisa would go home and go right back to work. No wonder she looked so trim. Her friend looked like she could eat a dozen lunches, and no one would notice. She worked very hard at training her horses, her stable was always full, and there was a waiting list of people who wanted her to train for them.

Lisa squeezed her arm. "It was fun today," she said. "Like old times."

"Thanks for everything," Alison said. "I mean that. Thanks, Lisa T. Jones. You are truly my best friend. See you soon. I'll work with Tigger, and I'll call you if I run into any problems."

"You've got a deal," said Lisa, and then more seriously, she added, "You are lucky to have so much to live for. Don't you forget that."

Alison frowned. "Yup, my life is one adventure after another, like the heroine tied to the train tracks." They both laughed.

"That's the trouble," said Lisa. "You are just like the heroine of one of your novels. You have one adventure after another. Think of all the adventures you have had in the past week. And remember last year when you told me about buying that gorgeous horse at some ridiculously low price? The one that turned out to be sound, instead of lame for life, and the owner was so furious, you thought he was going to kill you? How did you know, by the way? Oh, I know—the horse told you. I shouldn't have asked. Just be careful. I worry about you. Call me if you need me. Call me before you buy any more horses. Promise!"

"I promise," said Alison, crossing her fingers behind her back. "Don't worry. I'll be fine now. The security people will be here Monday, and Lady is always with me."

That evening Harry called her. "Did you hear? The police have charged all three of the men who broke into your house with robbery and attempted murder."

"Oh, dear! I'm so sorry for Fred and Moira Pollock," she said. "I expect the police will contact me about testifying. I don't look forward to that."

"Heard from Jack?" Harry asked.

"He left a message. It was something about something big. He can't get home for a while."

"Definitely not coming home before this weekend?"

"No, not a chance," she replied.

"Seen any more ghosts?"

"Only one or two," she said and laughed. She had examined that linen closet very carefully with the light on and off, but the door had refused to move.

"Well, in that case, my family's having a celebration for my dad's birthday at the Dog and Duck tomorrow evening. Would you like to join us?"

"I'd love to. So … how many times are we related?"

"At least once. It's a small town. My brother John has a family tree going back generations. I'll make a copy of it for you. Oh, and read *The Meadstead Lands*. We're all mentioned in there. I'll pick you up around seven."

She hesitated. "Harry … I'd better meet you there. People are talking about … you know … everything. And … well, my face is such a mess, and suppose your family doesn't like me?"

"I hear you've been out and about already, Mrs. Simons, and besides, my family's not like that. You'll see, but I'll meet you there."

The next morning Alison called Jack again, but there still was no reply. The greeting on his answering machine said to call back later; he was busy. *He's always too busy for me*, she thought bitterly. She tried sending him an e-mail, but it came back, refused. Where was he?

That evening Alison began a serious investigation of *The Meadstead Lands* book. Braving its small print, she read about the people who had settled around Roystone in Celtic times.

Originally, all the land around Roystone had belonged to one man, who sublet it to others, but by the fourteenth century there were at least eight families, called the Meadstead families, who owned the land in the small town and paid taxes to the king.

Alison took the book to bed with her. Fortified with a large cup of cocoa, she read on. It turned out that the Meadstead Lands were open lands, used by all. They were too precious to be owned by one person because of their access to water, and so their ownership was held in common, and their use was allotted to all landowners, according to an organized rotation. People who did not own any land at all were given permission to live and graze their animals on it. Then, around 1750, Parliament passed the Enclosure Acts that permitted the open (unfenced) land that had always been held in common by all land-owning members of a community to be placed into private ownership and be fenced. Pieces of land that had been divided into narrow strips and whose ownership was held by various landowners were joined together and fenced to become farms.

As was happening all over England, the Meadstead Lands were placed into private ownership, and each of the Meadstead families received an agreed-upon acreage that they then had the right to fence.

Was her property Meadstead Land? There were maps that were even more spidery than the text, and Alison's eyes grew heavy trying to decipher them. As she drifted off to sleep, she found herself wondering what happened to the people who were no longer able to live on the open land and graze their animals. Had they been evicted and left to starve? Had they become fodder for the cities and the Industrial Revolution? She came to the conclusion that, truly, the underpinning of all security in life was the ownership of land.

9

On Saturday evening when Alison arrived at the Dog and Duck Inn, it had a festive air about it. The door to the banquet room was open and the table set for ten. Harry and his father, Fred, and oldest brother, John, and his wife, Edith, were already there and they waved to Alison as soon as they saw her. Harry introduced her, and they all politely ignored the bruises around her eyes. She shook Fred Hastings hand, wished him a happy birthday, and gave him a box of chocolates.

Fred looked at her keenly and thanked her graciously, but Alison sensed from his hard stare that he wasn't sure about her.

"Alison, come sit next to us," Edith said. "We want to hear all about old man Johnson's colt. We wanted to buy him, but you beat us to it."

Alison laughed nervously. "Well, you'd be glad I beat you to it, if I told you what happened when I first brought him home. Your brother arrived just in time." Harry changed his place to sit next to Alison, and they both grinned at each other. "Shall I tell?" she asked him, but he shook his head.

"Do tell; do tell," begged John and Edith, but Harry, who never liked discussing details of his life and who had suffered much with his divorce, to their disappointment, shook his head again.

To change the subject, Alison said, "I've been reading the book on the Meadstead Lands that Harry gave to me."

"Good for you," said John. "Did you know that most of your property used to be Meadstead Lands? Did you know that subsequent to the Enclosures Act and until 1849, it belonged to the Hastings family?"

"Did it?" Alison replied. "I don't remember reading that." She didn't want to admit she had fallen asleep over the book.

"It's the small print," said John. "It defeats everyone. I told Uncle Ned that no one would be able to read it, didn't I, Dad? He wouldn't listen to me, and the maps are even more difficult." John took his reading glasses out of his pocket and put them on, tapping a finger on the table and imitating his uncle's quavering voice. "Now, boy, what's wrong with your eyes? Why, when I was your age, I walked five miles to school in the snow and five miles home."

Alison smiled. "He sounds like my granddad," she said. "Harry gave me some old newspaper clippings too. They said that the Hastings family gave John Trentham some land to build a house on for his fiancée, Elsie, but that Elsie Hastings married a James Forster instead. There was a description of the land, and it sounded very like mine. So I'm aware my land used to belong to the Hastings family, but I didn't know it was part of the Meadstead Lands too. How exciting!" But then, she shrugged her shoulders. "However, it was all such a long time ago."

"But we Hastings have lived here since 1066, and we never forget," John said. "We're always thinking about it, that it's still really ours."

Alison smiled again. She understood this passion for land. She felt as if it were part of her heritage too. "It's been up for sale several times."

"We were outbid every time, first by the Forsters after Trentham disappeared. Elsie loved that land, and her husband, James, was broken-hearted when she died, so he bought it in memory of her. The Forsters lived there for years, but then after your grandmother died, it was sold and purchased by Mrs. Brown, whose husband had been the manager of a local bank, and then finally you purchased it. We were outbid by bankers every time. This town used to be owned by farmers; now it's owned by gentlemen banker farmers!"

"Oops," said Alison. "It's true; my dad was a banker. And I suppose the Forster family were not part of the original Meadsteadmen, by any chance?"

John shook his head emphatically. "Not a chance," he said.

Harry whispered loudly, "I'll bet he'd let the Forsters be honorary Meadsteadmen if you let him graze some of his sheep on your back pasture, particularly as he's this year's honorary Meadstead constable."

"Tell him he has a deal if he'll throw in some lamb chops," Alison whispered back.

She and John shook hands on it. "Be careful," said John. "You're giving me permission to use your land."

"Oh, don't pay him any attention," said Edith. "He's obsessed with land and sheep." Harry made circular gestures close to his head, implying his brother's madness, and they all laughed.

"Ah, but it was Hastings land only 160 years ago," said John. "Maybe it will be Hastings land again someday … so the legend goes."

"Legend?" asked Alison, intrigued now. "What legend?"

"Oh, it's just a saying," said Edith. "It all started when the Hastings family gave John Trentham the twenty-five acres you own today. Please don't go on about the silly legend, John."

"It's not a silly legend," he argued. "It says that the land will never belong to the Hastings family again until a Trentham marries a Hastings."

"Rumors … gossip … just like the ghosts," Edith said, and then put her hand over her mouth, embarrassed. "Oh, I'm so sorry. I shouldn't have said that."

"I don't worry about ghosts," said Alison. "Really I don't. Please don't apologize. Please tell me more."

But it was then that Harry's brother Philip and his wife, Christina, and his sister Ellen and Allan, her husband, walked in. After the introductions had been made, Philip, who had overheard part of their conversation, said to her, "Alison, don't let John bore you with all that stuff about the land and the legend and the ghost."

"Please tell me," Alison begged. "What about the ghost?"

"That the house will be haunted until the legend comes true. Seen any of those white spooky things?" John replied.

"I haven't ever seen one," said Alison, thinking about the incident in the linen cupboard. Was that a ghost or just her imagination? She had come to the conclusion that a draft from the front door opening had caused the door to close suddenly when the men broke in to rob her. She had to admit to herself, she had never actually seen one, not even when she was a child. Now, however, her imagination—alive with ideas for a story since she had purchased *Gone Away*—was continuing to piece together the elements she needed. Now it had a house, a ghost, a legend, a love story, lies, betrayal, and a murder. All she needed to do was to find the key that bound them together. She sat silent, distracted, listening to the conversation as it swirled around her, but again and again, she found that most of her attention lay with Harry. She liked the sound of his laughter. *Are you the one, Harry Hastings, for my next book, my next hero?* she thought. He caught her looking at him and grinned. She hoped he wasn't reading her mind. Then she saw his father scrutinizing her, and she knew what he was thinking. *Don't worry; he's safe with me. I'll not hurt your son,* she thought. *I know Harry's divorce was a long and painful one.*

Fred Hastings sat at the far end of the table. He was a big man, overweight now, gray-haired and blue-eyed, with a weathered face. "Come on, everyone," he said. "Drink up. I may not be here next year. Enjoy it now."

Everyone toasted him, "Long life, Fred, and happiness."

They all enjoyed dinner and were drinking coffee and liqueurs when Moira Pollock walked in with the birthday cake that was alight with candles.

"Beth isn't here," Alison suddenly noticed.

"Oh, this is just a small party. Dad loves to party at the Dog and Duck for his birthday. It's his favorite place to eat," said Edith. "Tomorrow is the big event. All the family will get together at the farm, hundreds of us. We thought it might be a bit overwhelming for you. We wanted to meet you, though. Harry is always talking about you and your horses." She smiled at her brother-in-law, and he rolled his eyes. "You know how families are," she said.

Everyone sang happy birthday and clapped as Fred Hastings blew out the candles. It took him four or five tries to blow them all out, and his efforts caused him to erupt in coughing. "I can still do it," he said, his eyes watering.

What a family, Alison thought, and she envied Harry his brothers and sister. They were all so alike—fair-haired and blue-eyed. Except for Harry, they were all farmers and so comfortable with each other. She could detect no acrimony. The wives all seemed to get along well too. There was a warmth and a depth of shared good will that she had never encountered in a family. They were so unlike her husband's family. When she was first married, Jack's parents had shocked her with their unpleasant bickering. At first, she had laughed at their arguing, thinking they meant to be amusing, but that soon passed. She felt uneasy with their vindictiveness and began to avoid all contact with them. Her stomach was in a constant knot of anxiety in their presence.

Alison found herself studying Harry in particular, and every now and then, his hand closed over hers and gave it a reassuring squeeze.

"See? I told you so," he said quietly under cover of the buzz of conversation. "You're safe here."

They all wanted to know about her, her horses, and her books, but Alison's mind was running on a single track.

"Tell me more about the ghosts," she said to John.

"Well, the house is supposed to be haunted," said John, "by John Trentham. Probably just a rumor—something to do with that Elsie Hastings he was supposed to have married. What do you remember, Dad?"

"Just be careful," said his dad to Alison. "That house always had a reputation for having a ghost that walked. I remember when I was a lad—a long time ago—people talked about it."

"Does anyone know where Elsie and James Forster lived in Roystone?" Alison asked.

"They owned some property downtown. I have the information at home," John said. "I'll e-mail you tomorrow. Edith doesn't like me talking like this. Creepy, she says, all those happenings so many years ago to someone in our family."

Edith shook her head but said nothing.

"It was John Trentham I was mostly researching," John kept on. "Never could find out much. After Elsie was killed, I think he went to America and changed his name. That's why I kept running into a dead end. It was such a tragedy. She died very young in some kind of terrible hunting accident. Both Trentham and her husband were involved, but neither of them would ever speak of what happened."

"Now, John," said his wife determinedly. "That's enough." She turned to Alison. "He does go on and on. I'm sure everyone wants to hear about something else."

Alison longed to hear more details, but the conversation shifted to sheep, and she had to be content. She was beginning to feel sleepy anyway, and her bruised face was reminding her that it was time to stop talking. She was glad when Harry said, "How many brandies have you had, Alison? Come on. I'll take you home."

"Harry, that would be lovely. Your dad bought me one, and Mr. Pollock insisted on bringing me two, and I'm feeling quite tired. I think I'll accept your invitation, and get my car tomorrow, if you don't mind Lady riding with us. She goes everywhere with me. Somehow I feel safe with Lady."

"You'll be safe with me, too," he said.

"That's not what I meant," she said, embarrassed. *Will I be, Harry Hastings?* she thought. *Will I be? Do I even want to be?*

She said good-bye to everyone, feeling a little shy of Harry giving her a ride home, as well as what everyone must be thinking. But then she thought of what a wonderful family they were and how kind it was of them to have invited her to share this birthday party.

She collected Lady from her car and was silent part of the way up the hill, the dog sitting on her knee, and then she said, "You have a wonderful family, Harry. You are so blessed to belong—all your life, to belong."

"Am I?" said Harry quietly. It was then Alison remembered that Harry's wife, Julia, had left him, moving to London, taking the two little girls with her. She had heard that Julia was intent on marrying a wealthy businessman, to whom she was now engaged, as soon as the divorce was final. Her intent was to live abroad. Alison chattered on in uncharacteristic fashion. "Your dad had such a good time, too." *Why am I talking so much?* she wondered.

"My dad just loves going to the Dog and Duck," Harry said. It was the fact that he had wanted his dad to live with him, among other things, that had precipitated the divorce.

"And your mother?" Alison asked.

"She died of cancer five years ago. It came on so quickly—and she was gone." He abruptly changed the topic. "Jack home yet?"

"Not a sign of him. I've called and called his New York number, but no one ever answers the phone. I wish I knew where he was. You know, Harry, I don't think Jack likes living here. He says the town is full of eyes. I'm having the security system he wanted installed."

"Good idea but eyes?" he said and laughed.

He drove slowly up the driveway and parked under the trees that were losing their leaves. He kissed her slowly, experimentally, thoughtfully. "I like that," she said. She put her arms around him and returned his kiss, her heart pounding.

"Wow," he said. "I wasn't expecting that. Shall we try it again?"

"Not now. Not a game for us, Harry. I can't play at this," Alison said shakily, and then Lady jumped up and covered both their faces with kisses. "Oh-oh! My jealous dog is here … and my jealous husband may be waiting for both of us in the bushes."

Harry laughed. "And then I'd have to save you a third time. You are nothing but trouble, Alison Simons."

As he walked her to the front door, the new motion sensors picked up their movement, and all the outside lights turned on. "You're safe for now," he said, "until next time." *Not a game for me either*, he thought as she unlocked the door, and when she turned around, he was gone.

As she climbed into bed, her mind was on fire with ideas for her book, and her body was on fire with the memory of Harry's kisses. She began to giggle. Was it all the brandy or thinking about Harry? "Come on, ghosts," she said. "Where are you?" She waited and watched and listened intently, but within seconds she was fast asleep.

10

As the days went by, Alison thought about Jack less and less. Her writer's block finally gone, her mind was busy gathering information for the new book. She saved all her ideas, no matter when they came to her, onto her computer. Even at night, she climbed reluctantly out of bed, turned it on, and typed them out. Slowly, the book was beginning to take shape, but she needed more information. What had it been like to live in Roystone 160 years ago? She was fascinated by everything that she read and everything that John Hastings had told her about Elsie.

To her delight, he kept his word and e-mailed her the address of the house where James and Elsie Forster had lived. Alison drove by and was surprised to see it set in a beautiful neighborhood of older homes. She also was surprised to see how large it was and how much land surrounded it. It was a house made of cut stone, like her own, on at least an acre of land, surrounded by sycamore trees and a low stone wall. On an impulse, she parked the car in the driveway and knocked on the front door.

"Come in, lass," was the response when she had explained who she was. Mr. and Mrs. Tindall were delighted to meet her. "We've read all your books. Come on in, lass, and see the house."

Alison inhaled the sense of time in this house, for it was even older than her own home. She found there was an odor of dampness in the rooms that were closest to the river. There, the floors were a little uneven and, because of the tall narrow windows, a little dark.

The Tindalls, whose family had purchased it from the Forsters, showed her the old servants' entry, a small inconspicuous door in the front of the house that led from the outside world into the kitchen. They showed her the steep, wooden back stairs that led from the kitchen into the servants' bedrooms in the attic. How small the bedrooms were! They showed her the family's entrance, much bigger and grander, and how it led into a large foyer. She saw the dining room, living room, and the elegant curved staircase that led upward to the three large bedrooms and a bathroom. Originally, they explained, the two parts of the house were separate, connected only by a doorway from the kitchen that led into the family's dining room.

"Aye," Mr. Tindall said. "They were gentlemen that lived here then. Forsters, they all were. Women didn't vote in those days. Those were the days, weren't they, lass?"

"Oh, go on with you," said his wife. "Him and his old-fashioned notions."

"All the Forsters are gone away now, mind you," Mr. Tindall went on. "Too grand for this little town, with their fancy university educations."

So this was the house, thought Alison, *in which Elsie had lived and raised her three children.* It would have been a comfortable life, with a maid and a cook to help her. But did Elsie want this conventional life with James Forster, a man she did not love? Or did she long to be with John Trentham? Sadly, women didn't get to choose in those days—long before any kind of women's liberation, long before they had the vote, and long before, once married, they could own property. They obeyed their fathers, their husbands, and their families.

Perhaps Elsie helped her husband collect the rents from the tenants, for James Forster owned several pieces of property. Perhaps she helped with the accounts, for they had sold jams and clothing from a shop downtown. Perhaps she tried to obey her father, to raise her children, and to do her duty by her husband, although all the while her soul craved her lover.

The stable at the back of the property had been converted into a small, attractive flat, and all reminders of the horses and carriages that once had been kept there were gone. Alison tried to picture Elsie driving a smart carriage or riding her horse to hounds, but her imagination kept running into a wall. What had happened to her? Why had she died while she was so young? What was the tragedy?

And then, one afternoon, after struggling with the plot until the small hours of the morning, Alison found herself standing in front of the town's museum, a building that was far larger than she had expected, with its white columns and steps leading up to an imposing doorway. She noticed a brass plate that read "Built in 1848 with a donation from the Nightingale family." Once imposing, the museum now looked rundown and forgotten, perhaps a reminder of what might have been.

Feeling compelled, she opened the door and stepped inside and immediately came face-to-face with the large oil painting of John Trentham that was hanging in the main entrance hall. Until that moment, she had been unable to see him clearly in her mind. Now, she found she could not take her eyes from it. There were several other paintings of his close by, but she noticed none of them. The large self-portrait occupied the whole of one wall, and as she walked in the door, clumsily feeling in her handbag for money to pay for her admission, she could look at nothing else. He was standing, clad elegantly in riding apparel, as if he were going hunting, holding a pair of leather gloves in one hand. But what transfixed her was his expression. Afterward, all she remembered of the afternoon was standing before him, as if in a dream.

"Haunted, we call him," said Mrs. Rudd, the curator, whose frail appearance made Alison wonder if the old woman were as much of an antique as the painting—until she noticed the sharp eyes observing her and heard the strength of Mrs. Rudd's voice. "You can read all about him in the brochure. He were a bit like a rainy day—too bright too early."

"Yes," replied Alison, "perhaps that's what it is." But was he haunted? She thought his expression was something else—an expression of surprise, perhaps, the dark eyes alight with pleasure, and the full lips parting in a smile. She found it difficult to leave and decided to return the next day.

"I'm doing research for my book," she told Mrs. Rudd when she arrived the next afternoon. But this time, Alison looked carefully at all the other paintings. There was one in particular that drew her attention. It was of a very beautiful, dark-haired woman, dressed in an elaborate evening gown. She looked at the name and read "Mrs. Olivia St. James, wife of the mayor of Roystone, 1848." *A beautiful woman but the expression is curious,* she thought. *There's a hint of spitefulness in the smile. Is this the woman Trentham was accused of spending too much time with?* Rejected, Mrs. St. James could have made a cruel adversary. Her husband, the mayor, would have been a very powerful man in the small town.

Nothing else interested Alison, and she returned to the self-portrait. The longer she spent absorbed in the painting that afternoon, the more time she wanted to spend with it. Was it his eyes that drew her to him? While gazing at him, she had a sudden thought. The Nightingales had a John Trentham painting, and she had an invitation to visit them. That evening, she called them.

They were delighted to hear from her and insisted that she visit them the following afternoon. "We'll let the gardener know you're coming," Mrs. Nightingale said. "He and his wife have the lodge, and he'll make sure the gates are open for you."

The property was only a few miles, as the crow flew, from her own. She had driven past it many times without realizing to whom it belonged. As Alison drove through the wrought-iron gates, she thought what a magnificent home this was, with its circular driveway and immaculate formal garden. The stone wall that encircled the property looked as if it stretched for miles, and the lodge, larger than her house, was attached to the wall and stood just inside the open gates.

As the driveway approached the house, she stopped, opened her car door, and looked around her. The house was not quite as imposing as she had thought it would be. To be sure, it was a little severe—made out of brick, three stories high, with high, pointed gables, windows with shutters, and ivy winding its way up the walls—but sitting in the sunshine, it had a certain warmth to it. *It's a country house*, she thought. *It belongs here, and it's grown to be a part of the land.*

She walked up the steps and was going to ring the bell, but as her hand reached out, the door was opened by a neatly uniformed maid. To her delight, she heard the familiar Yorkshire accent. "They're expecting you, Mrs. Simons. Can I take your coat?" The house felt cold, so she declined and obediently followed the maid up the magnificent staircase that seemed to reach up to the heavens. The portraits of the previous owners gazed down upon them from every wall, and the ceiling was a painting of some kind of battle, involving horses and, she presumed, more long-dead Nightingales.

"Thank you so much for coming," said Dr. Nightingale as soon as Alison was announced. "We're in Barbara's boudoir this afternoon. We find the house a little cool in the winter, and this room is cozy. Please, call me John, and this is Barbara. Now, Alison, stand in the light, and let me take a look at your bruises. Don't be embarrassed. Yes, everything's healing nicely. Now come and sit in this chair in front of the fire."

"We're so glad to see you looking so well," said Barbara, though Alison could see she was examining the remains of the bruises around her eyes. "We've been so worried about you."

Alison thought the room was very elegant, with its white walls, wooden floors covered with Persian rugs, and windows clad in draperies that reached to the floor. There were four large armchairs arranged in front of the gas fire, and on two of the walls were floor-to-ceiling bookcases. In one corner, next to the window, was a grand piano, and scattered around the room were assorted small tables and chairs.

"Sit here, drink this, and tell us how your new book is coming along," Dr. Nightingale said as he handed her a large glass of sherry.

It tasted delicious, and Alison sipped it appreciatively. It was a chilly afternoon, and in spite of the gas fire, she felt the room to be a little chilly; she was glad she was still wearing her coat. Dr. Nightingale settled himself in his comfy-looking leather chair on the other side of the fire, with Barbara next to him. Alison hesitated to talk about her book, as it was in that stage when she found that sharing ideas could spoil her train of thought, but she was embarrassed to refuse their request. In the end, she said, "I'm sorry, but I can't tell you about my book. I don't talk about them until I write the words 'the end.'"

Barbara nodded her head in approval.

"Well, what do you think of our home?" John Nightingale asked. "My wife loves it, but I'm afraid it's too big for us these days."

"John wants us to move into the lodge, and he wants to convert the house into an hotel," Barbara said. "I keep telling him, it's our home that people would be staying in. Surely everything can't be based on money."

"Big houses are an expensive luxury," Dr. Nightingale said gently. "Things are a little difficult right now, my dear." Alison suspected he didn't want to have to tell her just how difficult things were financially. "Times are changing, and we must change with them." He turned to Alison and explained, "It was different in the old days. The family used to have parties at Christmas and invite the entire town. Everyone came to our little church and celebrated Jesus's birth at Christmas. We sang carols, ate parkin, and drank warm mulled wine. And then we celebrated harvesting the crops at the church and held the village fair up here.

But … the world has changed, Alison. People aren't interested in going to church. All people want these days are carnival rides and loud music."

"That man who beat you up—Ben Jones," Barbara said, changing the subject. "He rents from us, you know. Very disappointing. We've known his family for years. If we had known what kind of man he was, we never would have let him have that property, would we, John? His father was such a good man. What is the world coming to? Roystone has changed, I'm afraid, and not for the better."

Alison longed to disagree but wisely said nothing. Ben Jones and his friends, she was sure, were an anomaly and would spend a long time in prison for their crime. She accepted another glass of sherry. For a long moment, they sat in amicable silence, watching the gas fire as it flickered and struggled to keep the large room warm. She felt a draft and wondered where it was coming from and then noticed one of the windows was slightly open. Barbara was dressed in wool, but Dr. Nightingale seemed impervious to the cold, dressed in an open-necked shirt and slacks.

"We believe in plenty of fresh air," Barbara said, observing Alison. "John thinks it's healthy. He doesn't feel the cold, but I find it takes a bit of getting used to."

"All this is Nightingale land," said Dr. Nightingale suddenly, standing up. "See this map?" He showed her a map on the wall that detailed the land his family had been granted after the civil war, with the homes and farmland scattered over the county, now leased out.

"The Nightingales were very clever," Barbara remarked. "They were always careful to fight on the side that won."

Her husband shushed her hurriedly. "You'll confuse our guest," he said. "My family always has been on the side of what was right."

For a brief moment, Alison's eyes met Barbara's as she admired the map, and then she said, "I was wondering if I could see your John Trentham."

"Yes, my dear, yes," said Barbara. "Of course you can."

There, in one of the many bedrooms, down one of the long corridors lined with more portraits of Nightingales, was a small painting that took Alison completely by surprise. Was it the cold air that made shivers run down her spine, or was it this self-portrait? Her attraction to it was obvious, but she was oblivious to the curious stares of her hosts. The painting was similar to the one in the museum but much smaller and of the artist's head and shoulders only. She couldn't take her eyes from his large dark eyes and full red lips. The expression was different this time, she thought—much darker, as if he were brooding over something. There was something ageless about him, and she gazed in admiration until Barbara's small cough brought her back to the present.

"Painted later than the one in the museum?" Alison inquired.

"I don't know," said Dr. Nightingale. "Perhaps. It was sold to my father by your grandfather. You would have been a little girl then. What do you think of it?"

"Quite fascinating," said Alison. "I never saw it, that I can remember. I wonder why my grandfather sold it."

Barbara seemed evasive. "I don't know. It was all such a long time ago. We don't remember the details. Come on now, my dear. Let's go see the kennels and the horses. So much more interesting, don't you think?"

Alison went with them reluctantly. "Any chance that you might sell the painting?" she asked.

"My father promised that we would keep it in the family," John said gravely. "A promise he made to your grandfather. And I suppose we'll keep our word to him too. We Nightingales always keep our word, you know. We do what is right."

They left the house via a back door through a scullery that reminded Alison of her of her own, although hers was much smaller, and then walked across an open courtyard to the stables. The stables were large, with room for twenty horses, and were warmer, with fewer drafts than the house.

"The stables are relatively new," said Barbara. "Sandra, the gardener's wife, takes care of the horses and the dogs. She's reliable and takes care of everything for us. We want to be sure the horses are happy." The three horses seemed very happy and obviously were very well taken care of, as were the hounds. Everything was clean and neat—brass polished bright and the leather supple. *Owned with love,* thought Alison.

She looked carefully at the horse in the last loose box. "Isn't that Blue Velvet?"

"Ah, you recognized her. She came up lame after her winning race at Roystone. She'll be bred after Christmas to a champion sprinter. He should put a bit more speed on the foal."

What a good idea, thought Alison.

Later, as she was leaving, Barbara said, "We're looking to replace John's hunter. If you see one that looks suitable, do let us know, won't you? They are so hard to find these days. He needs a horse that's quiet, a weight carrier, one that likes to jump."

Alison promised to find one. People often called her with horses for sale, and this would be a wonderful home.

"And we'll be looking for a couple of racing prospects next year. I do hope you'll come to the sales with us," said Barbara.

*****

Dr. Nightingale watched as Alison drove away, but his reverie was broken when his wife said, "That painting affected her so strangely. Did you see her face? Perhaps the old stories are true. Her grandfather certainly thought so. If I had known they could be, I'd never have let her see it."

"Perhaps," John said thoughtfully. He had never particularly liked the painting, and it had been on his mind to let it go. With all their money tied up in the new conference center and with the stock market crash, they could use the cash. But that information, he thought, would break Barbara's heart, so he said nothing more. Still, he didn't believe in ghosts or anything spiritual. He was a doctor who had seen many people leave this world, and he had never ever seen any evidence of an afterlife. He simply thought that old man Forster must have had a very vivid imagination, as did Alison. *After all,* he thought, *she writes books ... and so does Barbara, for that matter.* He hadn't had the heart to tell Barbara that there would be no new racing prospects for several years.

11

As the days passed, Alison's mind and body began to heal. The memory of the savage attack began to recede, little by little. She thought about the people of Roystone and how they had lived all those years ago. She thought about John Trentham and visited the museum again and again. "I'm just getting background ideas for my next book," she told Mrs. Rudd.

That evening at the Dog and Duck, Mrs. Rudd said to Mrs. Crocket, "Background ideas. That's what Mrs. Simons tells me. 'I'm just getting background ideas for my next book, Mrs. Rudd.' She's at the museum every day and always the same painting she looks at. She's right obsessed with 'im, if you ask me. It fair gives me the creeps, the way she looks at 'im. Another gin and tonic, Mr. Pollock, if you please. Someone should warn her about that Trentham chap. He were too good-looking for 'is own good."

"But what shall I say to her?" Mrs. Crocket protested.

"Somebody should warn her," said Mrs. Rudd stubbornly. "It's only right. You know what they say about that house she's living in."

Each morning, Alison took advantage of the dry weather and worked with Tigger and rode Captain. Each afternoon, she visited the museum and gazed at the self-portrait. Every evening and until late into the night, she felt inspired and wrote more and more paragraphs, until the paragraphs grew into chapters. Now the plot of the book was falling into place, everything twisting and turning in her head—the families, the marriages, the lovers, the jealousies, and arcing overall was always the land.

She found a book in the library called *Roystone, Life in the Nineteenth*

Century, and she pored over its pages. She found it continued on where *The Meadstead Lands* book left off. The town, as she already knew in her heart, was in many ways the same then as it was now. Included in the book were drawings of the racecourse, the church, and the Nightingales' home. There were stories of the parties thrown by the Nightingale family at Christmas and summer solstice, to which everyone was invited. There was even the story of Elsie's death and a description of John Trentham's portrait in the town museum.

It was a small, close-knit, self-contained community, where people were born, lived, and died without ever leaving for the outside world. It was such a different world from her own. Young, single women never went anywhere alone—they were always chaperoned—and on Sundays, everyone went to church. Women had few rights, they could not vote, and their property belonged to their husbands. Both men and women who could not support themselves or who were in debt ended up living and working hard in the poorhouse, even when they were old.

Yet the more Alison researched the time frame of the 1850s, just after the Great Exhibition in London, the more she found to like about it. There was a sense of excitement in the air, as if anything were possible. England was a nation where life-changing discoveries were close at hand—a nation ascending, a nation on the cusp of power, with a great future. Even so, for most people it was still a quiet life, with musical evenings, gas lights, early morning risings, and always the labor of the land. Everyone knew everyone else—their neighbors, their friends—and they relied on each other. It was a time of great men and women writers, whose books she always had enjoyed. It was a world she could fit into very easily, for she always had felt a kinship with the slow pace of life closely linked to the land and its seasons. She liked the idea of silence, without the incessant ringing of telephones, the noisy intrusion of the television, and the smell of the automobiles.

Alison thought long and hard about John Trentham. She felt sure the townspeople were uncertain of this man. He was different, he was an artist, and once he acquired the reputation for seducing women, they would have ostracized him. After Elsie's death, he would have lived an isolated life on top of the hill, blaming himself and putting his very heart and soul into his paintings.

As she wrote, Alison felt herself slipping backwards in time. In all her imaginings, she had never dreamed of a story like this one. Nothing else existed for her. Everywhere she looked, instead of houses, she saw fields of barley. Instead of the noise of automobile engines, she heard the sound of the horses' iron hooves and carriage wheels on cobbled streets. Inside small shops or in the streets, she overheard the whisper of a conversation—two voices. Over and over, she heard a woman's anguished voice saying, "John, you betrayed me, and now I am to be married to a man I do not love. What shall I do?"

And a man replied, "I love you, Elsie Hastings. I was falsely accused. You are my only true love."

When am I living? Alison asked herself. In truth, she did not know, for she was living another life in another time, and it absorbed her. She saw the women with their long dresses and bonnets; the men with their tight breeches, jackets, high collars, and top hats. She observed their outward politeness to each other, their courtesies. And it was then she realized that beneath the controlled behavior, nothing was different from her own time. The passions, held tightly in check by the social code, were strong and deep, waiting to be unleashed. Was that what had happened to Elsie Forster and John Trentham? Had the longing, the desire for each other, finally overcome their fear of discovery?

As a writer, she always had lived her stories but never as keenly as this. Now, her imagination took flight. The walls that separated her from this world were down. Everywhere she looked, she saw John and Elsie and felt the power of their love. She felt alive, as Elsie had felt alive when she was with him. There was a strength to this love, and once she experienced it, she knew that it was beyond her control. It had the power to stir something within her, something she had written about many times but never experienced. John Trentham aroused an emotion within her that drew her inexorably back to the museum every day. He drew her closer and closer, as he had drawn Elsie closer. Alison felt their anguish when they were parted. She felt Elsie's despair when she was forced to marry a man she did not love, and she felt John Trentham's grief at Elsie's untimely death, when they were parted forever. All of Alison's own pent-up emotions were poured into the writing of her book.

It was then that the dreams began, dreams so vivid that she could not but believe they were real. It was neither Harry nor Jack in those dreams who came to her; it was John Trentham. Night after night, the same dreams. Night after night, she awoke to the memory, lying in the darkness, holding tight to her pillow, bathed in sweat. She was riding astride his horse, behind him, her arms clasped tightly around his waist. *We'll go south*, she heard him say. *We will go to a new world, where I own land. No one will find us there.* And then, always, something happened. She was falling, falling, and then darkness, and there was a barrier she could not cross.

Sometimes while dreaming, Alison found herself in her living room, walking out through the French doors into a garden filled with fragrant roses. John Trentham was there, waiting for her, sitting on an elegant chaise. She was wearing a green silk dress, and on her left hand was a ring, a circle of diamonds with a blue stone in the center, like a pool of blue water. And then, he was on one knee in front of her, holding her hands, gazing into her blue eyes with his dark eyes, and she could clearly hear him say, "*Not long now, my darling. It's almost our time.*"

"*I don't believe in ghosts*," she protested over and over.

"*Ghosts? Ghosts?*" he said, laughing. "*What ghosts? Come to me, my love, and know how real I am.*"

"*But I love Harry!*" she cried out.

"*You are my one true love*," he whispered. "*Our love is forever. Come to me.*"

For Alison, dream or reality, this world was so clear in her mind that she knew this was going to be her best book. She called Beaky and gave him the good news.

"Well done, Alison," he said. "I knew you could do it." They celebrated over the phone with a glass of wine.

Mrs. Crocket came two mornings a week, cleaned the house, and worked in the kitchen, baking Alison's favorite meat pies and scones. When she went home in the afternoon, sometimes Beth Durham came by, brought her knitting, stayed for an hour or two. The neighbors, like the Ospreys and the Allans, brought gifts of food and companionship. They knew Alison was writing a book, and they felt they were intruding, but they came anyway, because they cared about her and were concerned for her well-being. She was grateful for their company but many times hardly noticed them, being completely absorbed in her writing. They were surprised at the intensity of her concentration, but Alison reassured them it was always like this when she was writing. She knew she would remain like this until she finished the book. Harry called her every day, making sure she was safe and making her laugh. "I saw you in town today, buying groceries," he said. "You ignored me."

"Did I?" she said, embarrassed. "I didn't realize."

Sometimes in the evening, Harry came by with Beth and her husband, and they all ate dinner together. Alison relaxed, content and secure. She wrote as she had not been able to write in years. Lady was her close companion, always with her, always watching, and nothing escaped her keen eyes.

All the manuscript needed now was a title and a design for the front cover, and then it would be finished. She decided the front cover would be a photograph of *Gone Away*. This book had truly been a labor of love and rather an odd experience, even for her. Alison gave a sigh of relief as she e-mailed it to her publisher. Now she could forget all about John Trentham and his love for Elsie. Her life could move on.

But to her surprise, the dreams continued. Something had been aroused in her from which she could not look away. Instinctively—and to her horror—she knew what was happening. He was calling to her across time, and something in the depths of her soul was answering him. But why? Why was this happening to her?

During the day, when she was with Harry, she felt safe, complete. She laughed with him, looked into his eyes, and loved him, but night after night, she saw and heard John Trentham in her dreams. She was not afraid, but she took to sleeping with a light on. It changed nothing. She thought about calling Lisa and asking her advice, but realized she could tell no one about this. People in the town were already talking about her. If anyone found out about the dreams, she would be regarded as someone who had lost her mind. What would Harry think of her? No, she could tell no one. In desperation, she went to her doctor and begged him for sleeping pills. She told him she was exhausted from writing her book. He let her have a few, grudgingly, but she discovered they did nothing to help her. No matter how hard she fought, the dreams continued. "*I finished the book,*" she told him in desperation. "*I told the story. What is it you want from me?*"

"*You are my love,*" was his reply. "*My only love. I'm waiting for you.*"

"This is ridiculous," she said, clamping down vigorously on her imagination. "Waiting for me? Impossible!" She had to get over this.

She had to close the door to her imagination and get on with her life. But somehow, the door had opened, and now it refused to close.

Thoughts of Jack had faded from her mind. At first, she worried about where he could be and what he was doing. When she called his business, they told her he was well and still in New York. When she called him in New York, day or night, he was never there to answer the phone, and he never returned her calls or answered her messages. She began to think she would never see him again and contemplated filing for divorce.

Now that the book was complete, she was happily spending more and more of her time with Harry, and the pace of her life had quickened. It was almost Christmas, and Harry escorted her to the Horsemen's Association dinner and to all the other events that she had so longed to attend. Gossip abounded about them. What a handsome couple they made, everyone said, but she and Harry ignored it. They enjoyed the company of these people with whom they had so much in common, but they soon found they longed for other amusements.

"Let's go out of town," Harry said. "Let's go to the Highwayman's Arms for Christmas."

"Where's that?" she asked.

"It's up on the moors," he answered, "far away from prying eyes."

"What an odd name for a hotel. Hm-m-m ... far, far away?" she laughed. *Why not?* she thought. *Why not, indeed?* She deserved a long weekend out of town, especially one with Harry. She sighed dreamily. What fun they could have, far from anyone they knew. She was tired of only writing about love; she was ready to experience it. Away from home, she was sure there would be no dreams of John Trentham. She would sleep well, her body and soul satiated with lovemaking. She sighed with anticipation.

12

Jack, out of sight for so many months, now was completely out of Alison's mind. She was thinking joyfully about spending Christmas at the Highwayman's Arms and was happier than she had been in years. Her imagination ran wild and free. Harry was the highwayman. She was … she imagined endless scenarios. Could this be the beginning of a new book? She giggled. It had great possibilities. Every time she thought of Harry, her heart leaped with excitement. She was singing to herself, frying eggs, tomatoes, and sausages for breakfast and listening to the news on the radio when she heard Lady barking. *Strange,* she thought. *I've never heard her bark like that.* She heard a scuffling sound at the front door and then a familiar voice. Immediately, her peace of mind shattered and lay around her like shards of ice on the kitchen floor. Inside her stomach, she felt a familiar knot. She froze where she stood, leaning against the kitchen table for support.

"Alison? Alison, this damn dog won't let me in. What's going on?"

It was Jack. In the next instant, he was in the kitchen with her. He caught hold of her, turning her face from left to right, examining it carefully. "You're looking very well. Bruises all healed." Then he demanded, "Where did this dog come from? What happened to you? One of those damn horses kick you?"

Alison pushed him away and called Lady to her. She explained to Lady that this particular person was all right, no matter what he sounded like. Then she turned to her husband and said, "Hello, Jack. Did the police manage to find you, finally? I didn't. I've been calling you for months. Where've you been?"

"There were some messages …" he said vaguely. "I called, but you were never home, and so I just left you more messages. I would have come back, but I was negotiating the biggest deal of my life."

She said nothing; she just looked at him questioningly. She had received one message from him and that was weeks and weeks ago. She knew he was lying—but why?

"Alison, it's finally happened. I have incredible news. Something's happened. Something that I've been waiting and hoping for." Alison watched him in silence. It was years since she had seen him so wound up. "They did it—the Americans. They bought the company. They now own the biggest security company in the business, and I get to manage it." Jack's eyes blazed with excitement. "That's why I've been gone for so long. We can move south, back to civilization—they've even thrown in a house for us, a big house. Isn't that wonderful? We don't have to stay here one moment longer. I'll call the estate agent in the morning, and we'll put this mausoleum on the market. I can't wait to be out of here. Once we're in the new house, no one will ever know you wrote those awful books. That's where I've been all this time. Come on, Alison, I want to show you the home I've picked out for us. We can leave tomorrow. Let's start packing."

Alison looked at him in dismay. "But Jack, I don't want to leave here. Don't you want to hear what happened to me?"

"I thought it was that new horse? I thought the police mentioned a horse."

"No, it was a horse race. I won a lot of money. Three men broke in and tried to rob me. They tried to kill me." She was staring at him, trying to understand what was going on, why he hadn't come home, and why he had called only once.

"I don't suppose you were on your own?" he asked.

"What do you mean, on my own?"

"Well, were you?"

She was stung by his tone and didn't care if she annoyed him. "Well, actually, I wasn't alone."

His face darkened. "I stopped in town. People are talking about you. That's where you got the damn dog, isn't it? That vet?"

"So you knew all about it already."

"I just stopped in at the Dog and Duck for a drink. I heard all about it from the Pollocks. Their son is going to prison because of you."

In an astonished voice, she questioned him, "Because of me?"

"Because of you. Everyone saw you with that Harry Hastings, having tea at the races. They tell me you're an item now. Everyone knows he was here that night. Doing what, I'd like to know? What do people think about you after reading those books of yours? It was all right when no one read them, but now? It's disgraceful. You should be ashamed. I'd have thought after what happened, you'd be glad to leave!" His voice had risen until he was shouting.

She leaned over the table and shouted at him, "I'm not! I'm not!" But in spite of herself, Alison's voice faltered. She couldn't believe what she was hearing. "I like this town. I feel like I belong here. I'm happy you sold your business; I know how hard you've worked, but this is my home." She was feeling panicky, as if she were being backed into a corner.

"It's just a house, Alison," he said, sitting on a chair and deliberately rocking it backwards until it balanced on two legs.

"My family's home, Jack! My family's home for almost 150 years! My home, my town, my people—this is *my* home now. Something all of my very own!"

"Your home now? What about me?" He leaned forward now, with his arms on the table, and the chair crashed down. "Don't you ever think about me? It's always you and your horses and now, your dog, I suppose. I should never have agreed to move here. You think people will accept you, ever? They should ostracize you. You and those books. You're easy prey for anyone after they read that trash."

She was so stunned that for a moment, she was silent. Then she said, "You bastard. That's not true. People don't ostracize me, and I belong here. My books are not trash. How dare you call my books trash?" Now she was angry—really angry. She felt betrayed, almost the same as when she had recognized Ben Jones as one of her attackers. There was a lump in her throat and a pain in her chest.

Jack's expression changed. He was watching her closely. "It's that vet, Harry Hastings. He's at the bottom of this."

What did he hear? she wondered. *That Harry stayed the night?* She wondered what other news the gossip mill had provided. She and Harry had spent a lot of time together, but they were not lovers … not yet.

"Well, I'm not staying here, and neither are you," Jack spat out. "I'm your husband. You will do as you are told. We are moving to London."

Getting up, he grabbed her by the arm and began to hustle her up the stairs. "Start packing now."

Lady was waiting at the top of the stairs. Her lips drew back from her teeth and she growled softly as Jack pushed Alison up the stairs. Jack stopped and shouted, "I'm your husband and I have rights!"

Alison pulled away from him. "Things have changed, Jack. This is the twenty-first century. I have rights too. It's not just packing you're thinking about. And I've no intention of ever doing that again with you—not now, not ever. So keep your hands off me." Alison stalked up the rest of the stairs with Lady at her side and closed the bedroom door behind her.

Foxy, oh foxy, she thought. *Now I understand.* She was the fox in the painting, snarling, guarding her home from an intruder. And then she stood for a long time, looking out of the window at the sycamore trees and the valley, and as she stood there with her dog close beside her, she grew calmer. *How I love living here*, she thought. *How I love owning this land, with its memories of my granny and grandpa and the sense of privacy it has brought me. I'll never move. Never. No matter what happens.*

On the other side of the house were the stable and the horses. Beyond the horses and the barn were the pastures, and beyond the pastures, the stone wall that marked the boundary between her property and the rest of the world. Was that what Jack thought of her? That she was his property to do with as he wanted? Had anything really changed in the last 150 years?

It was if she had seen Jack for the first time. He thought that she wrote trash; he thought she was trash. When she married him, he had seemed so wise and knowledgeable about the world. She felt safe with him. He was her rock and her security blanket. But now, she wondered—had he married her for love or for her money? She had loaned him enough of her inheritance after their marriage for him to set himself up in the security business, a loan he had never repaid. He worked hard and had become very successful. At first, she ran the business for him, but after the business became successful, he didn't want her there. He insisted that she stay home, and all the while he spent more and more time at the office or out of town. Nothing she did interested him. It was almost as if she didn't exist. *Relegated to nonexistence*, she thought bitterly.

She thought she heard his car leaving but suddenly, Jack was in the room with her.

"It's that vet, isn't it? Are you sleeping with that vet?"

She could have told him the truth—that she and Harry were friends, not lovers—but out of perversity, sheer obstinacy, and fury, she remained silent. She simply turned her face away from him.

He stalked down the stairs, out of the house, and this time she heard the crunching of his car's tires on the driveway as he drove away.

She sat on the bed with her arms around Lady for a long time. *Believe what you like, and be damned to you,* she thought, but then, in the next instant, she was afraid. She felt as if she were an orphan all over again. She felt totally alone. She had been at the university less than a year when her parents had been killed. She still remembered vividly the sharp feeling of grief at losing them and then the shock at the realization that she was alone in the world. She had no money troubles, as her parents had left her their entire estate, which was considerable and included a home, and enough money to last her for several lifetimes, but there was no one for her to turn to. Even her best friend Lisa could not help her. Lisa had problems of her own. She was taking care of her mother who was ill, a barn full of horses, and a marriage that was becoming unraveled. That was when the bad headaches started. She couldn't eat or sleep. The only place she longed to be, her grandmother's house in Roystone, had been sold. It was the one place in her life where she had felt secure and happy and loved. Now everything and everyone she cared about was gone. She sank into despair and spent her days at the race track, any race track, or riding stable, where she could be around the horses.

That was where she had met Jack, at a racecourse where he was designing a security system. At first he was fun. He was kind and gentle, and with him she felt safe. He was always there for her, and she had to admit that without his help and the sense of stability he gave her, she would never have obtained her degree. At first, their marriage was a success. It was after his security business became successful that he changed. It became his life. It obsessed him. It was all he thought about and talked about. The more time he spent in London with his family, the stranger he became, until there was an intensity about him that frightened her. She had hoped that once they moved to Roystone, he might become once more the man she used to know, but if anything, he was worse, more silent, more secretive. And now his true feelings about her had surfaced. He thought she was trash! He thought her books were trash. She was overwhelmed. Feeling one of her sick headaches coming on that she hadn't had in years, Alison curled herself up in a ball on the bed, and with her dog in her arms, sobs shaking her body, she cried herself to sleep.

Three days later, Harry stopped by for a visit with a large brown envelope tucked into his jacket pocket. Mrs. Crocket met him at the front door.

"I'm so glad I called you, Dr. Hastings," she said. "Mrs. Simons isn't well. I'm worried about her. She's in bed with a terrible pain in her back and a sick headache, and she won't eat anything. My husband's been taking care of the horses, but we need some help. Come on in." She led him up the stairs to Alison's room and knocked on the door. "It's Dr. Hastings to see you, Mrs. Simons. Can he come in?"

"Just a minute, Mrs. Crocket," Alison said. Hurriedly, she sat up and wrapped her dressing gown around her shoulders. "Okay."

Harry peered around the bedroom door. Even though the room was in semi-darkness with the blinds closed, he could see how ill, how fragile, Alison looked. The bruises on her face had faded, but it was her eyes that haunted him. There was the look of a hunted animal in her eyes. Where was the woman with the laughing eyes? Where was the woman he loved? She had always been fragile, but this?

"My God, Alison," he said. "What on earth is going on?" He sat down on the bed next to her and took her in his arms, rocking her gently. She clung to him, sobbing. "Is your back hurting you again? You should have called me." *What on earth could have happened?* he wondered. "I made the reservation for four nights. Have you changed your mind? Is that the problem? I've been so afraid that perhaps you had changed your mind … anyway, when Mrs. Crocket called, I came right over." The black-and-white dog emerged from under the covers, barking with excitement, wriggling, and jumping up and down. "How's Lady doing?"

Alison wiped her eyes. "She's my best friend. You know that." She hugged the little dog and tears filled her eyes again. "Thanks for being here, Harry. I'm so afraid."

He held her close, rubbing her back. She clung to him, her body shaking. "What are you afraid of?" he asked. "Come on now. Everything's going to be all right, Ali. You're not to worry. I'm here. The police have them all locked up." He looked at her, and her eyes looked huge and dark.

Alison thought "it's been years since anyone called me Ali."

"You have, Lady," Harry went on. "Dogs are the best security system. What are you doing in bed? It's such a lovely day." Lady had her head on Harry's arm, seemingly beseeching him.

"Jack's home," she said, feeling oddly disloyal in spite of herself.

Hoping to extract a smile from her, he teased, "He's not under the bed, is he?"

But Alison was beyond humor. "No. He's not here. I don't know where he is. I hope he goes back to America and stays there. He wants me to sell this house and move to London with him. He's sold his security business."

"What?"

"Oh, yes, and he says my reputation is ruined and so is his because of my books. He says they're trash—I'm trash. He says everything is ruined, all because of me. Harry, I won't leave here. This is my home!" she cried out. "He says everyone in town thinks the robbery was all my fault. He says everyone should ostracize me." She sobbed and gave a hiccup. "All because I won that money at the races and my books."

"Rubbish," Harry scoffed. "No one I've spoken with thinks it was your fault. You know that's not true, and everyone loves your books. Don't listen to him. That boy of Fred and Moira's has been nothing but trouble for years. They packed him off to the navy in the hopes that would straighten him out, but it was no-go. He's going to end up in prison this time, Alison. The police have already called me. A trial date has been set for all of them. But Alison, what are you going to do? Are you going with Jack?"

"I'm not going with him anywhere. Not ever. I don't want to leave Roystone. This is where I belong … with you. Don't leave me, Harry. I'm so afraid of being alone. Silly, isn't it?"

"You'll never be alone, Alison. I'll not let you be alone," Harry said, looking into her eyes and then wrapping his arms around her. "You don't ever have to worry about that." He took a deep breath then and said, "Ali, I have a surprise for you. My brother finally gave it to me. I know your book is finished, but I thought this might interest you. Here." Out of his jacket pocket he produced a battered brown envelope.

While Alison opened the envelope, Harry opened the blinds and let the afternoon sunlight pour into the room. Inside the envelope were the original plans of her house; just as interesting, she found the Hastings and Forster family trees.

"My brother John had them locked away in the bank," Harry explained. "He said he thought you should have them now."

"You and your family are so thoughtful." She looked at him intently. "Harry, I have a surprise for you too. Turn around and look." She held her breath. *Will he like it,* she thought, *or will he be like everyone else and turn away?*

When Harry turned, he saw the painting that took up almost the entire wall—a life-sized portrait of a red fox, lying in front of the hollow entrance to a large tree trunk, a torn rabbit between its paws. It was looking back over its shoulder, its powerful teeth bared in a snarl at another fox in the distance. The frame was an old one, made of wood and painted in a soft gold tone.

He walked over and examined it closely. "It's magnificent," he said, ignoring the chills that ran down his spine. "I've heard of this painting. How did you come by it?"

"I inherited it from my father."

"It's another John Trentham. I've read about it somewhere—not sure where, but I've never seen it before."

"It's a dreadful picture," said Mrs. Crocket, opening the door wide. She had brought them a large tray filled with a pot of tea, cups, and milk, Cornish meat pasties, and homemade scones and jam and cream—Alison's favorite. "You look cheerful, Mrs. Simons. I see Dr. Hastings's visit has done you the world of good. Would you like tea up here or downstairs?"

When Alison didn't respond, Harry strode over to the door and took the tray. "This is much too heavy for you, Mrs. Crocket," he said. "Where shall I put it, Ali?"

"On the table here next to the bed," she said to Harry. "Thank you. So kind of you. I feel much better already." Her eyes followed Mrs. Crocket as she went down the stairs. When she was sure the housekeeper was out of earshot, she asked Harry, "Do you think it's magnificent? I keep it up here because most people are afraid of it."

"It's a wonderful picture."

"A wonderful picture," she echoed softly. She spread out the Forster family tree and looked at it intently. "So ... we are once-removed cousins, twice over."

"Second cousins," he agreed with a smile.

"Distantly related—quite distant," she said. "I'm glad. Aren't you, Harry?" Then she laughed.

He looked at the cups, as if suddenly noticing there was more than one cup on the tray. "Am I invited for tea?"

She laughed again, and he joined in her laughter. Still, her face was so white, except where traces of the bruises still stood out around her eyes. "Mrs. Crocket's put out two cups, so you must be invited."

They ate everything and drank the hot sweetened tea, with Harry sitting beside her on the bed. Together, they admired the picture of the fox and wondered if John Trentham had slept in this room, where he had kept the fox painting. They talked about the addition and all the improvements that Mrs. Brown had made. They studied the Forster family tree again, and then Alison unfolded the large piece of paper that was the Hastings family tree, going back ten generations. As she did so, a small piece of parchment, tied with blue ribbon and sealed with red sealing wax, fell out of it.

"Look, Harry. What's this?"

"I've never seen it before. Open it, and let's find out."

She pulled on the pieces of ribbon until they fell apart, and then she carefully unfolded the parchment and scrutinized the spidery, old-fashioned writing. She read slowly, struggling to understand the words. "It's a contract," she said. "Look, Harry. It's a contract that binds the Trentham and Hastings families for all time. It was never fulfilled because Elsie Hastings and John Trentham didn't marry. Is this where the legend your brother spoke of came from? The Hastings gave twenty-five acres of land to John Trentham. He gave Elsie Hastings a ring—a tourmaline surrounded by diamonds. How romantic! Have you ever seen it?"

"Oh, that would be the blue water. It's been missing for years."

Alison pointed to the Hastings family tree. "Look, Harry, here are you. You are not a Forster at all. You are 100 percent Hastings. But look here, the family trees have this portion in common, for twice the Hastings married Forsters. My grandmother was a Hastings, and she married a Forster." Then she said thoughtfully, "Harry, why did I not meet you years ago? Why did I not meet your brothers? Why did my grandmother never mention her family?"

"I've been talking to my dad," Harry answered, "and apparently they didn't want her to marry a Forster. There was such a scandal the first time. My dad says rumor had it that after Elsie was married to James Forster, she met John Trentham out hunting. Something went wrong. She was killed, and the ring, the blue water, as it was called, disappeared. That must be the ring in the contract. No one ever found out exactly what happened to the ring or to her. James Forster was suspected of foul play, but there was never any proof. Neither he nor John Trentham would ever say exactly what happened, although there were rumors that they fought over her."

Alison drew in her breath sharply. This was uncannily like the plot of her book. And the ring was like the ring in her dream. Was it just a dream? Where did her imagination get its ideas?

"My family, the Hastings family, had wanted your grandmother to marry someone who owned a farm that adjoined theirs," Harry explained, "but she ran off and married your grandfather, Robert Forster, instead."

"And what happened?"

"They cut her off without a penny and never spoke to her again."

"How awful!" Alison cried. "How cruel ... but those were hard times."

"Yes, they were. A lot of men were unemployed. The families wanted to join the farms for security. It has always been, as my brother John said, all about the land. It happened in the end but two generations later, because the properties were joined when my brother John Hastings married Edith, whose father owned the adjoining property. She was an only child, and her father, who had inherited the land from his father, left it to her in his will."

"Grandma never said anything, ever. She and my granddad were so happy together, but she must have missed her family." She thought for a moment and then asked, "Are all your family farmers, Harry?"

"All farmers and vets."

"The Forsters were bankers, shopkeepers, and landlords," she said, remembering, "and they all dislike animals, especially dogs. My grandfather and my father disliked them. My grandfather liked living here, though. He grew acres of fruit trees and had a jam factory. He liked living on the top of the hill, I think." She laughed. "Harry, I am the last of my kind."

"What do you mean?"

"Well, look at the bloodlines—I'm an only child, you see. My dad was an only child too. He was a Forster who was, like all of his kind, in business, and he disliked animals, dogs especially."

Harry gently touched her cheek with the back of his hand—the color had returned to her cheeks. "The last of your kind?" he said.

"I am, Harry. Look—I am Hastings, crossed with Forsters twice, but I am the only survivor, and I am a throwback to the Hastings side of the family in my love of animals, although I did run Jack's business for a while. *Oh, my,* she thought. *This is so, so strange. I can tell no one what I suspect. They would think I am mad!*

"As I recall my dad's stories," Harry said slowly, "your grandmother had a reputation for having a sixth sense with horses and a way with words. You are a throwback to her in that way. I wonder if Elsie also had those gifts. I suspect she had."

Alison's eyes filled with tears. "I was very close to my granny. How I miss her. She taught me everything I know about horses. I loved her very much and granddad too."

"How's Colossus?" he asked abruptly.

"Colossus?" she said, snuffling into a tissue. "He's with a trainer near York. He's doing very well. Ran second in a point-to-point in Northumberland. They've entered him in a little jump race at Wetherby, and if he wins that, they'll ship him over to Ireland, maybe to Clonmel. The trainer called me this morning and told me my silks looked good. He liked the color combination."

"He's entered already? Will you go and watch him?"

Actually, it had been an interesting conversation. Mr. O'Reilly had said, "Congratulations, Mrs. Simons. You were right. He's a natural jumper. He's not meant to be a hurdler. He jumps like a steeplechaser—his pedigree, you know, on the dam's side."

"Yes. I'm not surprised," she'd answered. So she had been right about the pedigree, and Colossus had been right about the jumping, but she didn't mention that.

When the trainer spoke again, his well-modulated tones were slipping, and she could hear a definite Irish brogue. "And Mrs. Simons, when he runs at Wetherby, would you come and watch him? And if he does well, would you consider entering him in a race in Ireland? And if he wins, there are a few horses I'd like you to take a look at with me while you're here and there."

"I'd be delighted," she had replied.

"Of course, it's more than just the jump. We'll have to see how much staying power he has and how much courage, but it's a grand pedigree, top and bottom. He's a fine horse, so he is, and I've found him a grand jockey."

Harry's voice interrupted her reverie, and her attention returned to him. "Alison? I said, will you go and watch him? In fact, let's both go to Ireland. I'll be in London the next couple of weeks, and I'll miss that first race, but my divorce will be final then." He stood up suddenly, watching the expression on her face. "It will give us both something to look forward to."

"Yes," she with determination. "Let's do it."

Mrs. Crocket's head appeared around the door. "I'm off, Mrs. Simons," she said. "I'll see you Thursday. I've put out some dinner for you both. Thought you might be needing something later."

They listened to her footsteps going down the stairs and the front door closing.

"Will you tell Jack where you are going?" Harry asked.

"Going where?" she asked him—she'd suddenly lost her train of thought.

"Can't concentrate, can you? Neither can I. We're alone, you know. How's your headache?"

"Headache's gone. Oh yes, I want to." She was looking at him, her heart pounding. "Yes, but not here. Let's go to the Highwayman's! What day is today?"

"It's any day you want it to be. Let's go," he said. "If Mrs. Crocket's left us a bottle of champagne, let's take it with us."

"I'll call her," said Alison, "and let her know we're going today after all. Her husband will feed the horses for me."

Before going to the Highwayman's, they first stopped at Harry's clinic and home. The clinic was closed for the day, but they could hear barking from the dogs that were boarded. The three-story brick house that was his clinic and home, at the end of a dead-end street, at first looked a little dark and forbidding.

But as Alison walked from room to room, she changed her opinion. "I like your house, Harry," she said. The high ceilings and the wooden floors made her voice echo.

"It's an empty house. Most of the furniture belonged to my ex, and it's gone with her."

"That's all right," Alison said, winding her arms around his neck. "How much furniture do we need right now? You do have a bed, don't you? We could go to the Highwayman's later."

"Oh yes," he replied.

*****

As Mrs. Crocket said to her friend Mrs. Pollock that Thursday evening in the Dog and Duck, "It were proper wonderful to hear her laugh like that with Dr. Hastings. Proper wonderful. I do wonder what that husband of Alison's said to make her so ill. He passed me going down the road, and him driving so fast he almost put me in the ditch."

"He's a right one," said Mrs. Pollock. "Never home, and every time I see him, he's in a bigger, faster car. He's in security? I wonder what he's securing. Serves him right. When the cat's away, the mouse will play. He's not taking care of his wife, and she writing those beautiful stories all by herself, and that lovely horse of hers. It just loves carrots. And my son attacking her like that. I'll never forgive him."

"Never mind," said Mrs. Crocket. "She's got Dr. H. keeping an eye on her now. I hope they enjoy the champagne I left out for them. What is the world coming to? Can you loan me your copy of that last book she wrote? I can't find mine, and they're all sold out at the bookshop. Been all sold out since it were all in the papers about the attack on her. Back-ordered too."

14

It was a long weekend that Harry and Alison never would forget. What a time they had, walking on the moors, for even the weather was kind to them. The sun shone all weekend and, with Lady beside them, they walked miles and miles through the heather, along peaty trails, looking for the icy cold pools of clear water called tarns.

"Let's run away," said Alison.

"Yes, let's," Harry said lovingly.

The Highwayman's Arms, a large old hotel that stood alone on the very top of the moors, was filled that weekend with Christmas revelers. No one took notice of Alison and Harry, and Harry and Alison didn't notice anyone else. They lived and loved in their room—a room they both thought perfect, as it was a suite with a dining area, a Jacuzzi tub, a tea maker, a refrigerator, and a small liquor cabinet. But best of all, it had a king-sized bed.

"This must be what heaven is like," Alison said. "I wish we could stay here forever." She found that her prediction had come true—on those nights she spent with Harry, there were no dreams; rather, she had the kind of sleep she had longed for. The next morning, when she awoke with a start, remembering the previous night, Harry was lying close to her. *What a novelty, not to awaken alone.* She reveled in it. How she loved this man. What a thoughtful lover he was. She put her arm over his chest, snuggled closer, and relaxed. This was what was missing from her life. She felt as if she were floating on a blue lake of warm water under a cloudless sky. Now the dreams would stop. She would be safe with Harry always, for it was if they had known each other all of their lives. They were comfortable together, completely at peace and secure in their love. Did she look into his eyes and know he was the one man she would love for all eternity? She didn't know. She didn't know why this question kept crossing her mind. The one thing she was sure of was that Harry was the man she was going to love for all the rest of her life. She loved him so much. When he held her in his arms, for the first time in a long time, she felt she was loved. What a glorious feeling it was to be loved. It was a weekend she would remember forever.

A call from Harry's clinic on Tuesday morning brought them both back to reality. "Time to go," he said. "My prescription for you is to keep riding and to take Lady with you. You'd like that, wouldn't you, Lady? If the weather stays like this, I could ride over on my old gelding, and we could go down to the sea next week. Have you ever done that?"

"I didn't know it was possible."

"Ah, well, we old Meadstead people know everything. We could ride over to my brother John's place. He and Edith are longing to see you again. Next week, I'll bring the Bear, and we'll go."

"The Bear?"

"My horse. Wait 'til you see him. He looks just like a big brown bear in the winter. And now, we must leave. It's the life of a poor vet for me."

*****

As Harry drove Alison home, he couldn't believe that everything was going so well for him. He thought of the amazing time they had spent together. Their lovemaking had aroused him in ways he hadn't experienced in years. "How many lovers have you had?" he'd asked her. But she had laughed and said, "I never kiss and tell. Shame on you for asking, Dr Hastings."

He sighed. His ex-wife, Julia, had never understood that he enjoyed being a vet in a small town. She had begged him to buy the house on the top of the hill. "It's the land," she had said. "We'll be somebody with that house, and there's room for a pool too." But Harry wasn't interested in money or big houses. His greatest satisfaction came from taking care of sick animals, making them well, and calming the frightened eyes of an animal in pain. He found he could stop the pain in others but not in himself. He found, too, that part of his calling was to rescue and heal those animals that been abandoned and find homes for them, and he did so willingly.

Somehow, he had failed Julia. He always had a guilty feeling that he could have done more, worked more, and tried harder to be the man she wanted him to be. Now he had lost her and his children. He used to dread going back to his empty house, but his love for Alison had changed all that, for he knew Alison was someone he could take care of and protect. For the first time in years, he had something to look forward to, and he whistled as he drove home.

*****

After that long weekend of lovemaking, Alison discovered that, as she had hoped, the spell was broken. She dreamed no more of John Trentham, and she believed herself to be free of him. The next week was a busy one for her. She spent it looking at horses for the Nightingales, testifying at the trial of Johnny Pollock, and avoiding the media who pursued her everywhere.

On the last day of the trial, when she stopped in at the Dog and Duck Inn on her way home after the case had gone to the jury, she felt much in need of a double gin and tonic. After the judge's criticism of her, she had found the trial most distressing and had left the court before the verdict had been brought in. Jennifer Standing was there waiting for her with a crowd of journalists. Alison had to admit to herself that this time she'd been successfully ambushed. She had no sooner sat down when she was surrounded by news reporters with cameras and microphones, all wanting to know her opinion of the sentencing of Ben Jones, the Pollock boy, and his accomplice. The jury had brought in their verdict.

Oh, Harry, where are you now? she thought.

"What's your opinion, Mrs. Simons?" asked Jennifer, her microphone at the ready. "Johnny Pollock and his friend have been given a suspended sentence. They are to be turned over to the navy, and Ben Johnson's been given a suspended sentence and probation, as a first-time offender."

What do I think? Alison was furious. She remembered the words of the judge—that she should have put the money in the bank, that it was an attractive nuisance, and therefore the attack was partly her fault. Supposing she had put the money in the bank? Would they then have killed her? Or tortured her? Where was her justice? After all, they had broken into her home, robbed her, and tried to kill her. She tried unsuccessfully to conceal her anger, but her face was white with rage.

"No comment" was all she would say, but in her heart, she remembered the lines in *The Meadstead Lands,* a book that had become her favorite bedtime reading. She remembered one sentence in particular: "Vagabonds are to be whipped out of town." Now that, she decided, would have been a much more appropriate punishment for those who had abused her and tortured her pony.

15

Alison had not seen Jack since their first encounter on his return from America, and his phone calls to her were so irate that she no longer answered them. Deciding it was long overdue, she called her solicitor, Mr. Stokes, and began divorce proceedings. She and Harry were spending all their time together, and if the town had eyes, they no longer cared. Alison was at peace, determined to go forward now with her new life. What she would do next depended on Colossus and how well he ran at Wetherby that weekend. She and Lisa were driving up there to watch the race. She wished with all her heart that Harry could go too, but he was involved with his children, saying good-bye as they moved to their new home in Bahrain.

Some roses had arrived and needed to be planted. She asked the gardener, Mr. Crocket, to dig up some of the grass to make room for them. Bulbs had arrived too—daffodils, tulips, and crocuses. In the spring, she would be able to sit in the living room and look out at a riot of color. Captain and Tigger were spending their afternoons out on pasture, and she enjoyed watching them running and playing, their winter coats so thick and long that they both had a furry look about them.

The manuscript was at the publishers. Now that she and Harry were lovers, she thought that she would be able to get John Trentham completely out of her mind. She made a vow that she would, but somehow, she couldn't. She no longer dreamed of him, and she no longer visited the museum, but he was still with her. To her surprise, she found herself talking to him, telling him everything about her life, even about Harry. *Am I obsessed with you?* she asked him. *Am I? Surely it can't be true.* It was like something out of time and understanding. After all, he had lived so long ago. And ghosts did not exist … did they?

She reasoned it was her book and all the research she had done. It was Harry who was her real obsession. Surely now the book was at the publishers and she had dreamed up the title, all thoughts of John Trentham would cease. It was to be called *Until the End of Time*. The contract that bound the Trenthams and the Hastings together had suggested it to her.

What a story she had written. Her imagination had taken wings this time. There was John Trentham, the young artist, so handsome that all the ladies were chasing him; and Elsie, so in love with him that she would look at no one else. Everyone who was anyone in town wanted him to paint their portraits, their wives' portraits, and their children's portraits. He was young successful, wealthy, and at the height of his powers. The Hastings family considered him quite a catch for their daughter. As for John Trentham, he had everything he could have wished for, including the land he had always wanted—twenty-five acres on the top of the hill where he could build a home for his bride.

And then everything went wrong. The mayor's wife, furious because she could not seduce him, accused him of bedding her. He went from flying so very high to being ostracized by everyone. He reputation was ruined, and then he lost his beloved, beautiful Elsie. Her family broke off the engagement and forcibly married her to James Forster, a man she did not love.

As Alison sat and gazed at her beloved fox painting, the ending of the book had come to her as easily as had the title. She thought of Elsie Hastings and how she had not been allowed to marry her true love. She pictured her, a pillar of the community, raising her children but secretly planning her escape. Her true love spent his time painting and waiting for her in the house on the top of the hill. Of course, she and John Trentham were secret lovers, and Elsie died tragically in a hunting accident after they met one last time. She was pleased with herself that she had managed to conceal from the reader the ending until the very end. There were so many possibilities that could have been drawn. Was it an accident? Was the husband involved? Had he seen them together and murdered Elsie in a fit of jealous rage? Had he discovered her riding on the back of John Trentham's horse and dragged her to the ground, where she had been trampled to death? The answer was not revealed until the last exciting paragraph, and Alison sighed with satisfaction. Beaky read it and loved it. He called her, and they celebrated over the phone this time with champagne. "Definitely your best yet, Alison. Where do you get your ideas? Is this a true story?"

"Of course not," she said. "Just my imagination, always my imagination."

"Well, it's perfect, and we're rushing it into production. And don't forget your contract, Alison. You owe us two more books in the next five years. If they are anything like this, you'll be able to afford to retire."

Alison was still celebrating with champagne when she called Harry. "My book's going to be out very soon, Harry. I'm having a book signing at the Antique Book Shoppe the evening before the race. Lisa and I are driving over to Wetherby the next morning. Don't come to the book signing, whatever you do. I'm not sending you an invitation. I'm afraid of Jack and his temper. He's furious about the divorce and the book. And for some reason I don't understand, he's particularly angry because I'm publishing it under my real name—Alison Forster—instead of my pen name. He blames you for the divorce. I've never seen him like this, Harry. Now he watches me all the time. No more trips to the Highwayman's Arms. I don't know what he'll do if he sees you."

"Not to worry; I won't be there," Harry said. "I think that's the same day my kids are going overseas. I'll probably be putting them all on the plane. Just be careful, Alison. Your divorce will be through very soon, sweetheart. Be safe."

Alison sent out invitations—elegant cards with the front cover of the book imprinted on one side and the date, time, and place on the other. She arranged for the music, refreshments, and posters and hoped she wouldn't sit there by herself all evening.

She didn't realize how many people she knew in Roystone or how many were interested in her book until she saw the queue that stretched around the building. To her surprise, once inside the door, she saw even more people, all waiting for her to sign their copy of *Until the End of Time*. There was even a sign that read "One copy only allowed. Additional copies may be ordered."

Beaky had insisted that she have the book signing at the Antique Book Shoppe, a place that was as large as a barn, and now she had to admit, he had been right, as usual. The place was full of people all listening to the music, eating the hors d'oeuvres, and best of all, buying copies of her book. Mr. Blake, the owner, had been thrilled when she called him and told him she wanted to hold it at his shop. "Thank you. Thank you, my dear. It's going to be such a success," he said. The publicity was just what his shop needed, and unbeknownst to her, he had placed a large advertisement in the local newspaper that read: "Meet the author. Alison Forster book signing this Saturday, 2–5 p.m. Refreshments will be served."

For a small extra fee, there was a video tour of her home and her horses, as well as photographs of Alison standing in front of the painting, *Gone Away*, holding the book. Jennifer Standing's young man, Alfred, had made the video, with Alison's permission.

The local chamber orchestra was playing Mozart, and the Dog and Duck had insisted on providing the hors d'oeuvres and the wine at a very special price. "A special price, especially for you Alison," said Mrs. Pollock giving her a big hug. Jack had wanted to arrange the security but she had refused, so he was just going to mingle with the guests, he said. Alison thought he was looking for Harry.

She was sitting at a table signing books, enjoying a glass of wine, and greeting friends, when suddenly Harry was standing in front of her.

"You're here," she said, startled.

"Nothing would have kept me away, Mrs. Simons."

"Now it is you who are nothing but trouble, Dr. Hastings," she said and added under her breath, "Jack's here."

"Is that why you haven't called me this week?"

Softly, she whispered, "He's watching me like a hawk. He wants me to go to London with him." Then, more loudly, she said, "You're not buying this book for yourself, are you?" Harry was positively gleaming that evening, she thought. She had never seen his eyes so blue.

"Don't, under any circumstances, go anywhere with him," he said quietly, bending over the table, and then he said loudly, "Of course it's for me. Why not?" His eyes were shining innocently. "Actually, it's for my brother John and his wife. They couldn't be here this evening."

"I'm so glad. I was worried you were going to read it."

"Is there something I shouldn't know about you, Mrs. Simons?"

"Harry," she mouthed. "You know there isn't." She tried to look cross with him but failed. "To whom shall I sign it? John and Edith?"

"You must be joking!" he said. "Sign it, please"—he lowered his voice so no one but she could hear—"from Alison, with all my love."

"Harry, not here," she said, her heart pounding, quickly signing her name and closing the book to conceal her words. "People are watching." And then she announced in a louder voice, "Next, please!" But she couldn't conceal her face that was flushed with pleasure.

*****

Jack watched Harry leave. He had waited and watched as Harry spoke to Alison. Alison's flushed face betrayed her, and now, Jack followed Harry out into the parking lot and quickly overtook him. "Stay away from my wife," he hissed, standing in front of Harry with clenched fists.

Although not a particularly big man, Harry was taller than Jack, and he tried his best to ignore him. He pushed past Jack, opening the door of his Land Rover. His two black dogs jumped out with wagging tails, glad to meet someone they felt sure was a friend. But Jack, his face dark with anger, was unwilling to back down, and he raised his fists. For a moment, Harry was unsure of the outcome, but Mr. Pollock, who was carrying food and wine from his van into the Antique Book Shoppe, saw what was going on and walked over to them.

"Everything all right, Dr. Hastings?" he asked, and Jack was forced to retreat.

"I hope so," said Harry. "I hope so.

*****

"I'm worried," Mr. Pollock said later, when he shared his observations of the encounter with his wife. "There's going to be trouble. I saw Mr. Simons's face. He was so angry. Is he staying here? If he is, I think we should ask him to leave."

16

Alison was over-the-moon happy. She and Lisa had watched Colossus win his first race at Wetherby by six lengths. "That was amazing. Did he tell you he wanted to jump like that?" Lisa had questioned her afterwards.

"Yes, in his way," Alison had replied thoughtfully. "His pedigree justified my belief that he would be a good jumper. And don't forget, he did jump his way off the Roystone racecourse over the rails. It was pure luck, though, that he was a winner the first time out."

Lisa hugged her. "Thanks for including me in your project," she said. "It's such a good idea. We're going to have so much fun. It'll be like old times." She got in her car and called out the window as she drove off, "Now, you be careful."

Alison felt blessed to have such a good friend who was willing to go in with her on what was, after all, something of a gamble. Racing horses would be a new life for both of them. She sighed. Although Jack was watching too closely for her to go safely with Harry to the Highwayman's Arms, she felt free to plan this new life. All she had to do now was wait for her divorce to be finalized.

In her heart, she was free from her husband and free of her obsession with John Trentham. It had all been a figment of her overactive imagination and her researching events that had happened to her ancestors. Now it was Harry who filled her thoughts and her dreams. She loved him so much. They were to be married as soon as her divorce was final She had even begun to look at wedding dresses—in blue, just like his eyes. She wanted to dance every time she thought of him.

One afternoon, as she was leaving for an appointment with her solicitor, there was a phone call from Mr. Grimes of the art gallery.

"I have a beautiful John Trentham here," he said. "It's on consignment. You've never seen it. No one has, and I know it will sell quickly. If you can, I think you should come today. The people from the museum are interested, and they're sending over an art expert tomorrow."

Alison swallowed hard. Could it be the self-portrait owned by the Nightingales? She could feel her heart begin to pound in her chest. John Nightingale had given her his word that he would never sell it. Could it be he had changed his mind? Still, her obsession with John Trentham was in the past. She was completely secure in her love for Harry, yet for a long moment, she hesitated.

Finally, Mr. Grimes said, "Are you there, Mrs. Simons?"

"Yes," she answered weakly. "I'll come by this afternoon."

"I've put it away for you. I knew you would want to see this."

Later at the gallery, Alison gasped when she saw the painting. It was the one she had seen at the Nightingales' home. She wanted it so much, yet she struggled with herself. She knew it was madness, but no matter how hard she tried, she could not resist the temptation to look at the painting again. And once she looked, she could not look away. She gazed as if hypnotized. "The Nightingales put this on consignment?"

"Why, yes," Mr. Grimes said. "How did you know?"

"I saw it at their home." She crossed her fingers and asked the price.

"Well, now, Mrs. Simons," he said, "you don't have to buy it, you know, but the amount they are asking is very reasonable." He actually thought the amount was outrageous. Dr. Nightingale had made him promise to get the price he wanted and to sell it to the museum, but Mr. Grimes knew there was no way the museum could afford to buy it. There was only one person who would be willing to spend that kind of money, and he had called her.

The price was exorbitant, but she gave him her credit card immediately. "I have a painting of a fox and also *Gone Away*, so now I have three John Trentham paintings," she said.

"I didn't know that," Mr. Grimes said. "You know, I think it'll be the first time since your grandfather's day that all of those paintings will be in that house together. Those were the very same paintings that were on the walls when Trentham disappeared."

"Disappeared?" said Alison, and then she remembered there was no headstone for him in the cemetery by the church. "What happened to him?"

"I don't think anyone knows. Who can remember? It was all such a long time ago," said Mr. Grimes. "But just be careful when you're on your own," he said. "There were rumors for years that the house was haunted in some way by those paintings."

"By the paintings? I didn't know that. Maybe my dad mentioned it once …" As she spoke the words, a memory crept to the edge of her consciousness but quickly faded. She would search for it later. Harry had said something, too, about the house having a "reputation." She didn't believe in ghosts. There had been that one strange incident when the linen cupboard door had mysteriously closed, but she had already dismissed that as a draft. She had told no one, not even her best friend, Lisa, about her dreams. She wished there was someone she could talk to. She was even tempted to tell Mr. Grimes about them, but it was impossible. Seeing the self-portrait had made her feelings for John Trentham stronger than ever. She fought against them, trying to put up a barrier high enough and strong enough to keep her safe. *Damn that imagination of mine*, she thought. It was completely out of control.

Mr. Grimes noticed the intensity of her expression. He wondered if he should have sold her the painting—it seemed to distress her somehow, and he held himself to blame.

"What do you think about the new shopping center and the new motorway?" she asked him suddenly.

"I know how you feel," he said, "but you've got to see it from our point of view. Roystone is part of the past; it's like a museum. The future is in the shopping center and hotels, and the new conference center and maybe even more gambling. There aren't enough people here to support my art gallery, and I want to retire soon. And we need the construction jobs. Unemployment is so high in this town right now."

Reluctantly, Alison agreed with him. "I suppose you're right, but sometimes I think we're losing something—our identity as a community, who we are. This town is so special to all of us."

"Ah, now," said Mr. Grimes thoughtfully as he placed the picture carefully in a box and wrapped it with paper. "You may be right there. I think like that too, sometimes, that there are too many changes. But what can we do? The shopping center's going to go in anyway, and the whole town has invested in it. Now, you take that picture home and enjoy it." He gave her arm a fatherly squeeze of encouragement.

The self-portrait was going home. She needed to phone John and Barbara Nightingale and thank them for selling it. She needed to let them know, too, about the horse she had found for them. With some training at Lisa's, it would make a steady hunter for John, and it deserved a good home like theirs. She wondered why they were selling the painting. Did they need the money to finance the shopping center, perhaps?

Alison was still pondering the question when she arrived home. She walked all through the house, trying to find the ideal place for it, but it eluded her … until she held it her arms, cradling it. Then, the place came to her immediately—in the living room on the wall opposite the French doors. As she held it up to the wall, she turned the painting around and noticed that something had been carved into the back of the frame. It was faint, and all she could make out were the words "I saw him." *How strange*, she thought. Then she shrugged her shoulders, hung the painting on the wall, and reminded herself she didn't believe in ghosts.

Even so, she had to admit that as soon as the picture was on the wall, she felt something different in the house—a feeling of anticipation, as if something were going to happen, something tremendous, something longed for. She felt as if the whole house was vibrating with excitement. *You are silly*, she thought. *Your imagination turns off for three years, and now it's running wild.*

The room needed a finishing touch, and then she remembered her grandfather's old shotgun. She wondered how it would look above *Gone Away*. She liked the idea and decided to ask Mr. Crocket to put it up there for her. Later that evening, as she sat in her favorite chair, gazing thoughtfully at the paintings, her mind began to wander again. She poured herself a glass of wine and although the room was warm, she lit the gas fire for company. With Lady at her feet, she gazed first at *Gone Away* and then at the self-portrait in the firelight as the room grew darker and darker. She still could not bring to mind the memory that eluded her. What was it? Something from childhood; something to do with the fifth bedroom; something to do with that night she was attacked—something it all had in common.

She remembered the family tree Harry had given her. It was so interesting that she had memorized all the names of her relatives, stretching back generation after generation. She had memorized Colossus's pedigree, too, going back ten generations. How many people knew their ancestors so well?

What a day it had been. First the painting, and then she had stopped by her solicitor's office and signed more papers for the divorce proceedings. They had decided that the grounds for the divorce would be unreasonable behavior. Mr. Stokes had assured her that it would go very quickly now, and she would be financially secure. "You were very wise to put the house in your name only, Mrs. Simons. Very wise. Not many women have such a grasp of business, keeping your income from your books separate from your husband's income. And you still have all the paperwork of the loan you made him. You just leave it all up to me," he said reassuringly. "I'll soon have it all finalized. And if necessary, we'll take out a restraining order against your husband."

Knowing that she would be financially secure eased some of the fear in Alison's heart; she knew that she could not go on living with a man she did not love. She stifled the tears that sprang to her eyes at the memory of the past weeks. Jack could not believe that she intended to go through with the divorce and kept showing up unexpectedly, harassing her and shouting at her. There were times when he insisted on sleeping in one of the guest rooms. She begged him to leave, to go to his house in London and live there, but he refused. He shouted louder, trying to bully her into giving him what he wanted, but that was impossible. She loved Harry now. "Be my wife," Jack kept saying. She shuddered at the thought of it.

Her mind wandering, Alison looked again at the hunting scene. What was it like to jump sidesaddle, to balance oneself with both legs on one side of the horse? Then she looked again at the self-portrait, her eyes flickering back and forth from one painting to the other.

And suddenly, everything fell into place. She recognized him. It was John Trentham, waiting on the far side of the jump for Elsie. It was Elsie, his love, on the chestnut horse.

And it was then she knew everything. They had never been lovers. He was still waiting—that's why the painting; that's why the house was haunted and what John Trentham was trying to tell her in the dreams. The painting was his way of remembering that last outing together—the last time when he and Elsie met, when she was killed, and when everything had gone wrong for him again. His love transcended time. *If only I could experience that love, a love that lasts forever,* Alison thought. She looked at the self-portrait and sighed. He looked so elegant and so sophisticated. Then she looked at the hunting scene. Such a beautiful black horse he was riding, just like Colossus.

Were they dreams I've been having? Or is John Trentham really waiting for me? Why me? And how? He's been dead for years.

Alison's mind was spinning. Harry was quite forgotten; it was as if he had never existed. She was so close to something, something she had always wanted. She heard a door upstairs open. And then she knew the connection, and her heart began to pound. She knew what the odor was. She had smelled it that night when the door slammed shut and locked her in the linen cupboard. It was the same odor that had made her faint that day all those years ago. She knew now what had been wrapped in the cloth in the fifth bedroom—but why were they there? Why had she never been allowed to see them?

Understanding flashed across her mind. She knew why her grandfather had sold one painting to the Nightingales. He understood the danger to her. He knew who she really was. This knowledge had been passed on to her father, and he had tried to warn her, but she hadn't listened.

The paintings had been carefully separated. Her father had inherited the fox painting. The self-portrait had been sold to the Nightingales. *Gone Away* had been sold to Mrs. Brown. It had been placed on consignment after her death, but eventually, by chance, it had returned to the house on the top of the hill. She wished she could talk to her grandfather, but she was too late. She wished she could talk to her father, but he was gone too. They both knew something that she could only guess at—her true identity.

Time. It was all about time. It was all about reaching back through the doorway of time to find out what had happened all those years ago. Alison thought about the generations. They were like waves on a beach, rushing toward the shore, each one finding its own way before being pulled back into the sea. She thought of the family tree that Harry had given her and tried to count each generation as it passed by, but the sound of the surf was in her ears, and the names kept getting jumbled.

Had not Mr. Stokes tried to warn her about something at the reading of her father's will, something her father had told him? She should get up and find out—she had a copy of the will in the safe—but her head was spinning. Was it the wine, or was she getting another sick headache? And then, instinctively, she knew what it was. She had butterflies in her stomach, and she couldn't quite catch her breath.

The three paintings were now in place, where they had been when John Trentham had disappeared. The doorway across time was opening. She could clearly see the hollow tree trunk in the painting of the fox. The fox was gone, and now the tunnel seemed to go on forever, twisting and turning until it reached into darkness and infinity. It was tempting her. Calling her. *Do I have the courage?* she wondered. *Do I have the courage to walk into time?* The logical part of her justified it. "I'll write a book about this," she said aloud, but it wasn't writing a book that she longed for. Her soul was yearning for this one man, her soul mate—the one man she could love for all eternity and who, in return, would love her. She felt so much desire for this man, and he was so close that she could feel his presence in the room.

What she was contemplating was dangerous, but she knew this was what she had always wanted, and she was willing to risk all to experience it. It was something greater than herself alone, something so profound that it shook her soul. It was a love and a passion that would outlast time.

She made a split-second decision. She took one step, and then another, and then another, walking forward into the darkness. "Wait for me, Lady," she said, turning, and then suddenly, looking back at that little black-and-white bundle of fur, she changed her mind. Lady was Harry's gift to her. She and Harry loved each other. She had promised his father she wouldn't hurt this man who was so vulnerable after his divorce. What would happen to Harry? Every step took her farther away from him and the life they were planning. She must be mad. She tried to turn back—but it was too late. She found herself being pulled down, down, down, sucked into the maelstrom of time. She struggled to escape, but the force was too strong for her, and she lost consciousness.

When she awakened, she was in her living room. The room was lit only by a few gaslights. On her left hand was a gold ring, a tourmaline surrounded by diamonds. Her dress was pale green silk. John was there!

He held out his hand to her, and she took it. He was exactly as she had known he would be. They looked into each other's eyes, and they knew each other, for time had changed nothing. Then he bent down and swept her into his arms.

"This time, forever," he said. "We shall never be apart again. We've waited for so long, Elsie, my own true love."

17

It was not one week but several, for it was almost March, before Harry and Alison were able to ride to the sea. The weather had been so miserably cold and wet that all thoughts of riding anywhere had been postponed. *February in England*, she thought and shivered. It was not her favorite time of the year. When she was home, she stayed indoors; the house always warm and cozy. They postponed the ride again and again, but when Harry heard that Colossus was entered for a race at Clonmel, he said, "Let's take a chance on some sunshine and ride over to my brother's place a couple of days before. We can leave the horses there. My brother won't mind, and Lady will have a whole flock of sheep to play with."

So it was early one bright, clear morning late in February that Harry pulled into the driveway with his horsebox and parked next to the stables. Alison was warming up Captain over some jumps while she waited for him. At first, she didn't notice his arrival; it was obvious she was enjoying herself. She and the horse were as one, their timing as they approached each jump so smooth that they made it look easy. Suddenly, she noticed Harry watching her and trotted Captain over to the fence.

"Where have you been?" she asked. "I almost gave up on you."

"Beth showed up at the clinic this morning. Her favorite dog was sick with a bowel obstruction. He's going to be okay, but for a while there it was touch-and-go. But I'm here now, and it's a beautiful day."

He opened the gate and leaned on it, waiting for her while she dismounted and led Captain into the stable. It was on her return that he received his first surprise. How different she looked! His second surprise was the slow look of appraisal she gave him. Was she cross with him for being late? He was going to take her in his arms but he hesitated. "Alison, you're looking very well. Where have you been? I've been calling you and calling you. I even came by a few times, but you were never home."

"Oh, I've been everywhere doing book signings. Beaky had me booked all over the country. The book is selling well, though, and as he said, I really need the money."

"Jack gone finally?" Harry asked hopefully.

"To London," she said, her voice sounding lower and almost husky. "Gone forever, I hope. Orders from the divorce court. I finally had to take out a restraining order against him. He's to leave me in peace."

"And Mrs. Crocket is …?"

"In the house. Her husband is coming by later to pick her up."

Harry heaved a sigh of regret—he wanted her so much—and then he looked at her again. This Alison was a different woman from the one he had been expecting to see. He took her in his arms and kissed her. For a moment, she hesitated and then, her body was against his, and their desire for each other was as it had always been. "I've missed you," he said huskily. "I've missed you so much, Ali." For a long moment, he was still, holding her in his arms, breathing in her scent, and taking his time in savoring being close to her again. "You look marvelous," he said in her ear. "Do you still love me? I love you. Let's leave Bear in the horse box." He began pulling her toward the stables.

"Won't he mind? Besides, it's so cold. There's frost on the ground."

"Bear has a hay net. I swear he won't even notice we're gone," Harry said, laughing and pulling her by the hand. Suddenly, he stopped and raised her hand, his eyes riveted on the ring. "Where did you get that ring?" he asked, his voice incredulous.

"It was given to me."

"Given to you? That looks just like Elsie's ring. Remember? The one in the contract? The one that was lost the day that she died. It was a blue tourmaline surrounded by diamonds. Did you find it somewhere?"

"It was a gift from someone … recently, long ago … in a different lifetime," Alison said, her face white. She stood, not looking at him, twisting the ring around and around on her finger.

"Recently, long ago?" he echoed. He said nothing more, holding her away from him with his hands on her shoulders, looking at her intently. She refused to meet his eyes. "What do you mean, a gift?" he asked her. "Is there someone else? Have you met someone else already?"

"Please don't be angry with me, Harry." She spoke rapidly. "I … I had Mr. Crocket hang my granddad's old gun on the wall over one of the paintings in the living room, and he found the ring. It was in the wall, all covered over. It's so beautiful. I love wearing it."

"Is this true? You found it, or did someone give it to you? Don't lie to me, Alison. Don't ever lie to me. I couldn't bear it." He took hold of her chin, tilting it up, forcing her eyes to meet his.

"I'll never lie to you, Harry. Please believe me. I swear there's no one else," she said, her eyes filling with tears.

When he looked into her eyes, her eyes held him. It was like looking into pools of deep blue water; down, down he swam into their depths. What were they saying? Something came over him, clouding his judgment, clouding his mind. Suddenly, the ring was not important to him, and without another word, he let her go, turned around, walked to the back of the horse box, and led out Bear.

"He does look like a bear," Alison said, looking at the large brown gelding. "Look at that coat."

"I don't clip him, and it's colder on the other side of town," said Harry, and then he hesitated.

Alison watched him intently. Now it was if she were holding him apart from her, as if a barrier was between them, and Alison could see it was one he could not climb over.

He finally said, "What will you do now?"

"I'll never leave this house, Harry. I'll stay here forever. I belong here." Alison looked at Harry. It had been a mistake to wear the ring, but it was so beautiful, and she enjoyed wearing it. It lightened her spirits whenever she looked at it. Was her decision to spend this weekend with him a mistake? No, she owed Harry this weekend. She and John were agreed. It was but one weekend to them—they who would ride the waves of time for all eternity—and she and Harry had loved each other so much. She sighed.

*****

While Harry was putting the saddle and bridle on Bear, he kept turning around to look at Alison. Who was this woman? He felt he'd known the "other" Alison all the way through, but this Alison? Did he know her? She had softened—her eyes, her face, even her hair was different. Perhaps it was her voice, deeper and throatier. No, it must be the eyes, he decided, for there was a new expression to her eyes. Her hair looked longer and it was in curls. He was more fascinated than ever. But where was the Alison he had known—the Alison he'd spent four wonderful days with at the Highwayman's Arms; the Alison at the book signing; the Alison whose life he had saved twice; the Alison who had looked at him with real need in her eyes?

"Harry," she said. "Please don't be jealous about the ring."

"Jealous? It's just a ring," he said ruefully, and then he laughed at himself, for in truth, when he was with her, nothing else mattered. He watched her swing herself into the saddle and call Lady. This Alison was a self-confident woman who no longer had any unanswered questions or any fears ... but then he thought he was mistaken. Of course, he was. It was the same Alison, but there was something different. What was it? It had to be her eyes. She looked at him with different eyes, eyes that were so blue and so calm.

He wondered what a life with her would be like. It would be intense, always, and it would be a life of instant decisions, not for the faint of heart. For a moment, he almost sympathized with Jack, and then he remembered their lovemaking, her kisses, her laughter, and the joy he felt being with her, and he thought Jack a fool.

They took turns ponying Tigger as they cantered and trotted along the edges of fields. They rode onto property Alison had not explored before. She had not realized how much land there was on the other side of her stone walls. Harry pointed out some of the land that had belonged to the Hastings family for centuries. They could still see where, in olden times, the fields had been long and narrow so that when the horses plowed, they would have to turn at the ends fewer times.

It was as if they were stepping back in time into a world where there were no tractors or noisy machines. There were horses and plows and the songs of the birds in the fields and hedgerows. It was a world that Alison found familiar and enjoyable.

They reached the end of the fields, and then there was only a gate that lay between them and the sand and the sea. After they were through it, they followed a path that led down to an empty beach, and they could smell the salt from the sea and the surf. The tide was out, and all that was before them was the hard golden sand.

Harry said, "Take off Captain's tack and let him go."

"Are you sure, Harry?" she asked.

"Yes, let him go. He'll have a wonderful time. It's a small, enclosed beach, and he won't go far, as long as we hold on to Bear and Tigger."

Captain galloped down to the water as if it were the most familiar thing in the world to him to run through the surf and the waves. He ran and played and ran some more before returning to them. Watching Captain intently, Tigger was alive and longing to run. Harry held on to him tightly. He had no intention of releasing him yet.

Alison offered a carrot and caught Captain. He was sweating and breathing hard; his legs were wet with sand and the cold of the sea was up to his belly. Quickly, she put back on his saddle and bridle and held onto his reins before they let Tigger go. Harry slipped off the halter, and they watched as he trotted away, head high and tail over his back. "Lovely movement," said Harry. "Yes, Alison, he's another winner. He has a sweet temperament now too."

She smiled at him. "I can always pick the horses, Harry."

He smiled back and had to agree. "Come on," he said. "Let's keep Tigger company." She climbed on Captain and followed Harry as he rode Bear down to the water. Together, they cantered along in the shallows at the edge of the sea. Tigger joined them, urging them on. Harry let Bear choose his own pace, faster and faster, until all they could hear was the drumming of the hooves. Alison watched Bear, with Harry crouched over his back, and Tigger and Lady ahead of her, and the curve of the sky, and the land. Finally, she pulled up. Captain was breathless and so was she. She slid off his back, leaned against Captain's side, laughing and offering him a carrot.

"That was so much fun," she said. "Thank you."

Harry rode Bear over to her, grinning. He dismounted, caught Tigger, and put his halter back on. "I think he's finally tired," he said. He looked at Alison. She was so intensely alive, so warm, so close to him. For a moment, he was tempted to let all the horses go and head for the nearest sand dune with her, but a look from her, a laugh, and a shake of her head stopped him, and he swung himself back onto his horse.

Alison caught the intensity of his gaze and understood him exactly— they each knew what the other was thinking. After a rough beginning to their day, they were back in sync with each other. Bear was enjoying himself, dancing in the shallow water at the edge of the sea and skittering sideways at the birds. Harry sat easily on him, anticipating every move and laughing at his antics. He had dropped Tigger's lead rope, but Tigger just stood there, tired but with his head high, his sides heaving.

She called out, "Did I tell you that Mr. O'Reilly wants us to meet his family tomorrow? They are so excited about Colossus, and he wants me to look at more horses—for him to buy this time."

But Harry couldn't hear. The tide was on the turn, and the sound of the surf drowned out her words—and he was thinking of other things.

Suddenly, he rode up next to her and leaned down. "Let's do this again soon, before the shopping center is built and all the people come."

"Let's," she said. "Soon." She looked at him steadily. "You know, I love you, Harry Hastings. Trust me as I trust you in everything. Always be here for me, won't you?"

He dismounted and looked at her, his heart in his eyes. "You know I'm here for you always, but you are trouble, Alison Simons. You know that?" He thought he would give her a leg up onto her horse but being so close to her, he could not resist—he turned her around, caught her around the waist, and lifted her up against him. To his surprise, she put her arms around his neck and answered his kisses with a passion that left him breathless. He thought, *To hell with the horses*, and then he was oblivious to everything except her closeness. She seemed aware of his urgent need, and he felt her body respond, when an unexpected wall of icy cold water surged around them. Captain skittered away, pulling on the reins, and they both almost lost their balance and fell over.

*****

"Harry …" Alison said breathlessly. His kisses tasted so sweet. She was sure now that she was doing the right thing by having this one last weekend with him. What a life they could have had, but she had made her decision. *Is it too late to change my mind?* There could be no turning back, for yet another part of her perceived the dimensions of this one small life as so narrow compared with the existence she was now experiencing.

Harry laughed and threw her up onto her horse. "This weekend, Alison Simons, nothing will come between us. I will be the highwayman, and you will be …?"

"Ah, who will I be? Not Alison Simons anymore. You'll have to wait to find out who I am." Looking down at him, she laughed. "And you'll have to catch me first. I'll race you to the road."

She had a head start and despite Bear's best efforts, Captain arrived at the road first. He needed no encouragement, as he was thinking about going home for dinner. "Let's go see your brother. I'm hungry," Alison said. "I'm looking forward to a proper Yorkshire tea."

They rode along a narrow road where the branches of the trees met over their heads and where the sound of the horses' hooves were muffled in the brown dirt beneath their feet.

"It's still here," said Alison. "This is part of the old way from Roystone, the one the coaches used."

"Yes, how did you know?" Harry asked, surprised. "It used to go to Burnham and then onto the moors past the Highwayman's Arms, but it was abandoned years ago. When John inherited the farm from my dad, he decided to clear this part and make it usable."

The road they were on curved gently until it joined the main road, and in a few minutes, they could see the valley with its farmhouse laid out below them.

"Beautiful," said Alison.

"When John married Edith, it was what the families had been wanting for years," Harry explained. "Her father owned the land next door to my family, and they were able to create one large farm. My brother Philip, my sister, and I thought it an excellent idea."

"You were raised here, Harry?"

"Yes, although John and Edith have made so many changes, I hardly recognize the place.

Alison saw a large stone farmhouse, with chickens foraging in the front yard. Alongside of it was a large barn, and she saw two brown horses grazing in a field behind. There were a few acres of what looked like young oats and turnips, but everything else was grassland and sheep, as far as the eye could see. The fields were neatly divided into squares and rectangles by dry stone walls, and in the distance, she could make out what appeared to be a tarn, the surface of which looked gray and stormy.

"Come on," said Harry. "See those clouds? It's going to rain any minute." While Harry was closing the gate, Alison, with Lady close by, led Captain and Tigger toward the stables, where they were met by John and Edith. "Hurry!" said Edith. "Here comes the rain. Let's get the horses into the barn. There are plenty of empty loose boxes, and we put out hay for them. There's plenty of water and food for Lady, too. We put our dogs in a couple of the loose boxes while Lady settles in."

With the horses and dogs in the barn and taken care of, they all made a run for the house, shedding boots and jackets in the scullery. The rain was coming down steadily now, and the wind was blowing it in squalls against the windows. The extra large kitchen felt warm after the cold of the wind, and Alison looked approvingly at the fire roaring in the fireplace, the table set for tea, the flagstone floor, and the big stainless steel cooking range.

"We were wondering where you were," Edith said, giving Alison a hug. "It's so late. John was just about to set off in the car to look for you. So nice to meet you again."

"How kind of you to say that." Alison was touched by Edith's generous nature. "We've had a wonderful day. I'm stiff, though. It was a longer ride than I'm used to."

Harry agreed. "I'd forgotten just how many miles it is," he said.

"I envy you your barn," said Alison to John.

"It was built years ago," said Harry, "when all the barns were made of stone—the houses too."

"Have you seen the price of the barn conversions?" asked John. "With a bit of work, we could probably sell the barn for more than the house."

"If my brother John could flip barns instead of houses and make a profit, he would," said Harry.

John punched him on the arm playfully. "I listen to Dr. Nightingale," he said. "You should too. Philip's doing very well. He just sold a cottage not far from here. He made some money on it, I can tell you."

But Harry shook his head. "I have my clinic, and that's enough for me. Besides, I hear Nightingale has overreached himself and may be in financial trouble." John shook his head and would have none of it.

"So that was the famous Tigger?" asked Edith. "I hear Harry rescued you from him."

Alison looked questioningly at Harry. He grinned and said, "They pestered me until I told them all about Ben Jones. He should have been sentenced to ten years instead of getting probation. I hear he's home again, and his landlord is trying to evict him." And then he went on, turning to Alison. His face looked suddenly grim and his voice stressed. "We're all worried about you, Alison. Ben Jones should never have been turned loose."

"There's no need for you to worry, Harry," said Alison quietly, her eyes focusing on him, calming him and easing his fear. "I'll be all right. I have Lady now, and the security system is in."

"And we're worried about you, Harry," said John soothingly. "Any time you want, you are always welcome to live here with us."

"I'm all right," said Harry, but he looked at his brother with gratitude. "You never know; I may take you up on it yet, come lambing season."

After a moment, Edith asked, "How is Tigger now? He looks lovely."

"He is lovely, and he enjoys pulling the cart," said Alison. She had forgotten about Ben and the way he had treated Tigger. It seemed like such a long time ago—a lifetime ago. Alison glimpsed something through the doorway into the living room, and as she walked out of the kitchen, her gaze fell on the picture that dominated the room. It was large, four foot by five foot, and it depicted three shire horses pulling a harrow. Everything was curved—the land, the horses, and the sky. Alison was drawn into it and for a few minutes, she was completely absorbed and could say nothing. Finally, she said, "Another John Trentham?"

Edith nodded, and then Alison said to John, her eyes still fixed on the painting, "Did you ever plow the land with horses?"

"No," he said. "Come on and sit down. We've set the table in the kitchen. It's the warmest room in the house. Edith'll bring the tea. I've always had tractors, but my dad did plow with horses, as did his father before him. I still have one Shire horse, but he's retired now. We used to go to the fairs, and he pulled a big carriage and gave rides, but people aren't interested anymore. All they want to do is go on the Ferris wheels. It's a sign of the times, I guess."

How sad, thought Alison, and then she looked out the window at the fields and the sheep. "Do you ever get lonely?" she asked Edith, who was bustling around with the teapot.

"Lord, no," Edith replied. "I don't have time. Now Harry, let the tea brew for a minute. I teach at the local school during the week and then on weekends, the family stop by. It's civilized here now, but when John and Harry were growing up, it was very different. The house has been modernized several times. It must have been a hard life, a hundred or so years ago, living out here so far from town. They used to have ovens on both sides of the fireplace, and the fire was always going, even on days when it was hot. There was no electricity, just gas lights—and remember the outhouses?"

"Like my house used to be," said Alison, remembering, "but I suppose it depends what you are used to. People lived for centuries without computers or television."

"I couldn't live without my dishwasher," said Edith.

"Nor I mine, yet there were other compensations," Alison replied dreamily, looking again at the painting of the horses plowing. "That oneness with the land, the rhythm of the seasons, the planting, the harvesting, the horses, that sense of belonging—everyone belonged to the land."

"But women couldn't vote," Edith argued.

"How many times have you voted recently, Edith?" asked Alison.

"You're right," Edith laughed. "I suppose you had to do a lot of research for your new book."

"Oh yes," Alison said quietly, "a lot of research, but I think I would have liked that way of life, in the right circumstances, with the right man. No shopping centers, just the land and the sky and the horses." Edith looked at her strangely. Alison suspected Edith would have hated that way of life and all the hard physical labor. "And your boys?" Alison asked. "Will they take over the farm one day?"

"Derek will, but Keith will be a vet, like his uncle Harry. They're both away at school right now. We're all farmers and vets in this family. You should get John to show you the little cart he's kept stored in the barn. No one's used it for years, but it might fit Tigger. It's a dog cart that they used to drive into town."

"The roads are too busy for dog carts," said Alison.

"True, but before you go, you should take a look at it. It's very elegant," she replied.

But Alison was noticing the bookcase, which held copies of her books. "You've read my books? I thought Harry was just teasing me," she said in surprise.

"Of course we've read them," said Edith. "I read them aloud to John in the evenings." She stared at Alison for a moment, as if trying to decide whether to say something. Then she said, "You know, you don't seem to be the same woman we met at my father-in-law's birthday dinner. The change is remarkable. You look so healthy, so strong, and so secure." She lowered her voice and asked, "Has Harry caused these changes?" Before Alison could reply, Edith asked, "And your ideas. Where do they come from?"

"I get them at night when I'm sleeping," Alison responded, "and the next morning I sit and tap away on the computer." She found Edith's close examination of her disconcerting, and changed the subject abruptly.

After they had finished the ham sandwiches, homemade scones, clotted cream, and jam, they toasted Colossus's win at Wetherby and Alison's new book with a bottle of homemade plum wine.

"What's your book called again?" asked Edith.

"*Until the End of Time*," said Alison. "I'll send you a copy. I hope you enjoy it. It's a little different, a historical romance with a murder."

"I know we will. We always enjoy your books. What did you think of it, Harry?" said Edith, looking at him sideways. "He was supposed to have brought us a copy from your book signing, but so far, we haven't seen it."

"It was lovely," he said plainly, gazing at Alison with adoring eyes.

"You don't have to go home tonight, Alison," Edith said. "Please stay. We have plenty of bedrooms, you know, and we'd enjoy your company."

"I wish I could, Edith, but my solicitor's bringing me copies of some papers I need tomorrow, and he's determined to see me before I catch the plane. But thank you, Edith. It's so kind of you to offer, and thank you for keeping my horses and my dog for me for the weekend. I know they'll love staying with you. Lady looks quite at home already." After they finished eating—ham, sandwiches, scones, custard slices, and the pot of tea—Alison suggested they go back out to the barn. "Please show me the dogcart," she said, "and I want to say good-bye to Lady and the horses before we leave, and then I must go home. But that was what I call a proper Yorkshire afternoon tea. Thank you, Edith, it was quite lovely. I won't ever forget this."

*****

As soon as Harry and Alison had driven away, Edith said to John, "Well, what did you think of her today? I wouldn't have recognized her. And as for Harry, he was fascinated by her."

"Well, she is fascinating," said John, feigning a sigh.

"What do you mean?"

"Nothing. I just agreed with you dear." He grinned. "But she is a real catch."

She shooed him out of the kitchen and called her sister. They had a long chat about her brother-in-law and his new girlfriend. "Not only is her new book a big success, but they're off to Ireland, racing horses this weekend."

"What it must be like to have money," her sister commented. "How does Harry look?"

"Well, Harry looks tired and a bit thin, but she just looks marvelous. She was sort of radiant. He couldn't take his eyes off her, and neither could John. I don't know what it is—her hair, maybe. And you should have seen what she was wearing—the most elegant divided skirt I've ever seen and long leather boots. But even more interesting, she was wearing a ring with a blue stone on her left hand. John said it looked like Elsie's ring, the one that went missing all those years ago. It was strange that she was wearing it."

18

Jack hated living in the north country. At first, he had enjoyed living in the house at the top of the hill, particularly as it was Alison's money that had purchased it. But now he felt people were peering into his life—"nosy parkering," he called it. He longed for the anonymity of the big city and was sure once he persuaded Alison to go back there, where he could keep a close eye on her, everything would be all right. He longed to get Alison somewhere where no one knew she had published those dreadful books. He would make her use a different pen name, and their address would not be given out to anyone. He would design a special security system for the home. No one would get in or out unless he knew about it, for he thought, ominously, things could not go on as they were.

If he could get her to see the new house, he knew she would love it. She'd forget all about getting a divorce and wanting to live in this musty old museum, full of ghosts of long-dead Forsters. *Ughhh*. He hated it, and he hated that fox picture. It gave him the creeps. *That disgusting dead rabbit*. He had always thought that fox looked hungry and somehow predatory. He was going to get rid of the picture—lose it in the move, together with that dog.

He thought if his mother threw a party with a gift for Alison—a ring, maybe, of some kind—she would come to London with him. Once away from here, they would never come back. He wouldn't let her come back, and then he'd sell everything.

And so he stayed on at the house in Roystone, first shouting and threatening and then cajoling her. In the past, he had always been able to bend her to his will, but now, to his surprise, something had changed.

Now, she stubbornly and tenaciously refused to do his bidding—and there was another problem.

Alison was no longer afraid. No matter how much he shouted at her, she was no longer afraid. He didn't dare try anything, because that dog of hers was always watching him so closely. What was it she'd said to him? "I wouldn't do that, my dear. Lady's here." But there was something else—he couldn't quite put his finger on what it was. There was a change in her; not just the lack of fear but something else. She had refused to stop the divorce and soon it would be final. She had signed the papers, and the terms were a disgrace. She would have half of his money—half of all the money he had worked so hard for all these years! How could this happen to him? It was all his! It had to have something to do with that vet, Harry Hastings, or maybe that damn dog he had given her. It was more like a familiar than a dog. It even slept on the bed next to her, where he should have been.

She looked so well too. She looked younger and healthier than he ever remembered. He didn't know how she was doing it, because she was writing another book. What else could she be doing, wandering around half the night? And where was she during the day? He had refused to leave and was sleeping in one of the guest rooms. Every night he meant to stay awake and ask her what she was doing, but he always fell asleep. One morning, a neighbor called to complain about the noise. "We heard dogs barking and the sound of people laughing, and we saw lights coming from behind your house."

Nosy neighbors, Jack thought. He hadn't heard anything. Mind you, he had never liked any of the neighbors, nor had he ever liked this house or living so far north. It was so cold in the winter, and there was no one he could really talk to. The men in the Dog and Duck were all farmers, albeit "gentlemen farmers," and he had a hard time understanding their accents. They bought his security systems, but he had a feeling they were laughing at him behind his back. No doubt his wife's disgusting books were the cause of their laughter.

And just this past week, she'd taken out a restraining order against him. Against *him*. She had told the judge she felt threatened by him. How dare she? And the judge had agreed with her. He was to have no further contact with her. He was forbidden to enter the house even—his house. He'd intended to spend the weekend in London, enjoying his new home and his mother's party. But at the last moment, he decided that he had to come back one last time and persuade her to go with him. The house on top of the hill was dark. He knocked on the door, but no one answered. If she wasn't home, where was she?

Jack turned off all the security alarms and let himself in the front door. There were suitcases in the entryway. So she wasn't far away. Was she going somewhere, maybe with that damn vet? He was going to find out. He hid in the scullery and waited. He was glad he'd left his car at the Dog and Duck and walked up the road. Now he'd have it out with her one last time and he waited impatiently in the darkness.

*****

Alison fell asleep with her head on Harry's shoulder on the way home. He put in the gate code and the new electric gates opened. He drove up to the front door and gently kissed her awake.

"You're home," he said.

She yawned and stretched. "Are we here already? Come on in," she said. "I have something to show you."

"How could I refuse such an invitation, Alison, my love?" *Are you my love?* he wondered.

Together, they opened the front door and stepped inside. She turned on the lights. "How dark it was without electricity," she said.

It was months later that he remembered her remark and wondered at it.

"Suitcases packed already?" Harry observed.

"In case I sleep in," she said. "I have something to show you." She led him into the living room and turned on all the lights. "Look, Harry. My grandfather sold it to the Nightingales. He didn't want me to have it, and neither did they."

There, on the wall, was another John Trentham—the self-portrait he had seen at the Nightingales' home many times. He saw her admire it lovingly and felt jealous.

"Be careful, Alison," he said in sudden fear. "This house has a reputation; the artist had a reputation too."

"As do you, Dr. Hastings," she laughed at him. "As do you."

"But still," he said, "no smoke without fire." He was still jealous.

"I have something for you," she said and handed him a sealed envelope.

"Don't open it until you get back to your brother's. Promise me. I owe you so much, Harry—my life, twice. Thank you for sharing yourself and your family. For the first time, I feel like I belong."

"Of course you belong, with me. I love you, Ali, but you owe me nothing," he said and kissed her again.

"We mustn't awaken the sleeping ghosts, must we?" she said and laughingly pushed him away. "Besides, my aged solicitor will be here at 8 a.m. He's bringing over some papers for me."

"He's coming all the way out here? Old man Stokes? I thought it was his son who was going to be here."

"Old man Stokes is coming. He wants to see my John Trentham paintings."

Harry laughed. "You've bewitched him," he said, and he thought, *You've bewitched me too.* He looked into her eyes. How clear they looked this night.

"Now go," she said. "I'll call you if I have any problems."

"Promise me," he said, but suddenly, he felt uneasy. Something cold at the base of his spine was warning him. Was someone else—not just the ghosts—watching them? "Alison, I'll leave my dogs with you, just in case," and he fetched them from the Land Rover. "Now, you stay with Alison," he told them. "John and I will be here in the morning." He drove away, thinking that as long as the security system was turned on and she had the dogs, she was safe. The Pollocks were keeping an eye on Jack for him. Jack had been drinking and talking far too much at the Dog and Duck. Everyone was looking forward to his leaving town and never coming back.

*****

Alison locked the front door as Harry drove away and then checked that the security was all turned on before walking up the stairs with the two dogs. "Come on, girls," she said. "Let's go and climb into bed. I am so tired."

*****

Jack heard the sound of tires crunching on the gravel and knew that the car was moving away. He couldn't see anything, because the scullery windows were on the other side of the house. *Whose car was that?* he wondered. He opened the scullery door into the house, holding a whip he had found hanging on a peg on the wall. He slapped it experimentally against his hand, enjoying the sound it made, and crept into the kitchen. Now he had something to use on her and on that damn dog too, if it got in the way. He thought about Harry and almost licked his lips at the thought of what he would do to the vet if he found him with her. The rich bitch! He almost laughed to himself. He was going to make her pay tonight. And he had all night to do it. He had every right to be here, no matter what that judge said.

The house was almost completely dark, except for a few small nightlights. He stood still, getting his bearings, ignoring the sudden temperature drop in the room. Then, in spite of himself—for he was rigid with anger—he shivered. It was so cold in here. Didn't she ever turn up the central heat or light the gas fire?

He crept quietly through the kitchen before going up the stairs. His intention was to take her by surprise in her bedroom. *What was that?* he suddenly wondered. In the semi-darkness, movement caught his eye. He stood in the doorway and sucked in his breath in sudden fear.

A figure was drifting silently down the stairs. It was Alison! Jack watched her walk toward him out of the darkness and into the pools of moonlight that shone through the thick glass of the front door. At her heels were two large black dogs. She was dressed in a weird outfit that he didn't recognize—a long black skirt and red jacket with a black hat. Her eyes were wide open, looking at him—no, looking through him. He was going to say something, do something, but she didn't see him, and he changed his mind. He watched her, fascinated, as she glided down the winding staircase and then turned the corner into the living room. He followed her, still holding his breath, as she went quickly to the French doors, opened them, and stepped outside.

He exhaled slowly and then drew in another breath. *What is happening?* There in the moonlight were hounds and horsemen. They were gathered outside the Dog and Duck Inn. He could clearly see the name on the sign ... but how could that be? The Dog and Duck was miles away. There were so many people, so many men in red coats, and so many horses. The women were all riding sidesaddle. And the noise—there was so much noise. Dogs were barking, people were talking, and horses were whinnying with excitement. The people on horseback were drinking something out of cups, and he could hear them asking for refills.

As Alison stepped outside, a man came forward. It had to be that damn vet! And yet this man was so much taller than he remembered, and he had black curly hair. They smiled at each other and as in a dream, he watched as they exchanged greetings, held each other so very closely, and kissed. On and on, they kissed. How passionately they kissed. Jack ground his teeth in fury.

The man helped Alison mount her horse sidesaddle, and then he raised a horn to his lips and blew. At the sound, Jack startled. His eyes fell on the shotgun over the painting. He was there in one bound, and dropped the whip in favor of the gun. Turning, he made for the open French doors, raising the gun to his shoulder. How dare she be so happy! How dare she! She had tricked him all along. She was leaving him all alone, and all he could hear was the sound of their laughter. It seemed to mock him, and somehow his finger tightened on the trigger. There was an explosion and then silence. There was only the moonlight as it streamed over the grass and in through the open door.

Had it really happened? He ran outside and almost fell over her body. She was lying there, so very still on the ground. He knew she was dead. There was so much blood. Next to her were the bodies of two black dogs. Of the hounds and the huntsmen, nothing remained.

It was then that the cold penetrated to his heart. The air was so cold around him that he could see his breath. He was afraid to the marrow of his soul. What had happened? He knew only that he couldn't stay a moment longer. Jack turned and ran out the front door and onto the driveway. The door, seemingly of its own volition, slammed shut behind him. He ran, shaking, not caring about the blood on his shoes or the footprints he left behind. It was then he realized what he had done—he was still holding the shotgun … and his life was destroyed. It had to be that vet's fault, and he was determined to make him pay for it.

*****

Harry drove back to his brother's home and walked into the kitchen, dropped the envelope onto the table, and put on the electric kettle. He was whistling. He was happy for the first time in weeks. Perhaps it was the happiest day of his life. Remembering how he had felt being with Alison made him smile. What had she given him? He opened the envelope. To his surprise, there was a copy of Colossus's papers, a contract of some kind, a check for five thousand pounds, and a note. The note read: "He won at Wetherby. I've signed over a half interest in him to you and half of his winnings. No expenses to you, Harry, just a half interest in his winnings forever. Trust me. I love you. Alison."

He was stunned. She owed him nothing. Nothing. He ran to the phone. He had to talk to her—this couldn't wait until tomorrow. The phone just rang and rang until the answering machine picked it up. *Where is she? Something is wrong.* Where was his brother? He ran into the barn. "John, something's wrong with Alison. She's not answering the phone. John, I'm so afraid."

As Harry drove up the hill toward Alison's home, and John was calling the police on his cell phone, they unknowingly passed Jack, who was hiding in a ditch along the road. "Something's wrong. The gate's open!" Harry shouted. He accelerated in sudden fear and stopped abruptly at the front door. "Quick! Quick!" he cried out.

He rang the doorbell and hammered on the door. No one answered. The house was in darkness. No dogs barked a welcome. No lights turned on. "Something's wrong. Something's wrong!" he shouted to his brother. "I should never have left her." He ran to the Land Rover, found a tire iron, and used it to break the window into the kitchen. He felt around for the catch, cutting his hand, and then opened the window and climbed inside.

"Alison! Alison!" he shouted. He ran through the house, turning on all the lights, and then he went up the stairs, two at a time. *Where is she? Where are the dogs?* Her bedroom was dark, and her bed felt empty and cold. He ran back down the stairs, noticed the French doors leading onto the garden were open. He turned on all the outside lights. It was then that he saw her, with the dogs lying next to her on the grass. He ran to her, and when he saw her, his soul was chilled and hope left his heart. He gathered her up and held her in his arms, blood staining his shirt.

"Alison, Alison, all my fault. I should never have left you. Please forgive me!" he cried out. "Alison, my love, don't leave me. Please don't leave me. Oh, my God, I've lost you all—all my girls, forever." Outside, there began a howling—it was Lady, who knew that she had lost her love, and in the distance, Harry could hear the wailing of the sirens from the police cars.

19

The police found Jack running down the road. He was still carrying the shotgun. He was arrested and later charged with the murder of Alison Simons. Some months later, he was tried by a jury of his peers. His fingerprints were on the shotgun and powder residue had been found on his hands and his face. The whip had been found on the floor of the living room with his fingerprints all over it, and his words—shrieked to the jury, over and over—confirmed their suspicions. He was guilty of an exciting crime of passion that they would remember for the rest of their lives. It was much better than anything they had ever seen on reality television, and crowds lined up every day to see the trial in person. Despite Jack's claims of madness and his desire to be convicted of nothing more than guilt by reason of diminished responsibility, the jury looked carefully at the evidence and found him guilty of murder. There was the ample evidence of the gun, the whip, and of malice aforethought, as he had broken into Alison's home and lay in wait for her. After the judge sentenced him to ten years, there was an outcry from the entire country, for many thought he should have been given life in prison.

In the months leading up to his trial, Jack's testimony, which was leaked to the press, caused quite a stir. It made the local news, the national news, and then the international news. "It's that house!" he had screamed. "Haunted! Should be pulled down. It was the vet—all the vet's fault." Over and over, Jack repeated the same mysterious story. He saw Alison walking downstairs dressed in a long skirt and a red jacket. She walked to the French doors, opened them, and stepped outside. Immediately, he could see that it was daylight, outside the Dog and Duck Inn. There were so many horses and dogs and people, all milling around. He saw her walk up to a man, who was tall with dark hair. She kissed him! How she kissed him! It was disgraceful—his wife, kissing some strange man. Then he helped her to mount her horse, sidesaddle. Jack thought it was Hastings. Who else could it have been? There was so much noise and confusion—the dogs barking, the sound of people laughing, and so much excitement. Under questioning, Jack admitted he'd dropped the whip in favor of the shotgun. He swore that he didn't know it was loaded. Then, there was the explosion, and everything went black. Yes, he and Alison were getting a divorce. Yes, he admitted that the court had told him not to go into the house. Yes, he'd had a few drinks at the Dog and Duck—though he couldn't remember how many. Yes, he knew that the neighbors, the Ospreys, had complained about the noise of dogs barking and people partying late at night. All Jack could manage to say over and over was, "I know it was him—that damn vet. She was leaving with him. Her suitcases were packed and in the hall. But how did the Dog and Duck Inn get behind my house and all those dogs and people and horses? I swear I didn't know the gun was loaded."

The neighbors, the Ospreys and the Allans, testified to strange noises and lights recently, but no one had actually seen anything. They had heard the sound of raised voices over the past months, though it was always Jack shouting at poor Alison, and she the sweetest young thing anyone had ever known, and him leaving her alone so much. An attempt was made to show that he had been behind the first attack on Alison after the races, but it was never proved.

When the trial made the national news, Jack's life became public knowledge. His fiancée, Anne, whose father owned the security company that had purchased Jack's company, testified for the prosecution. Under questioning, she volunteered that she and Jack had been engaged for six months. He had been promising to marry her as soon as some "business" in England had been taken care of, and she believed she had had a narrow escape.

20

Alison's will caused quite a stir locally when its contents became known. The news traveled the small town like a wildfire. She had left her entire estate—her property, her home, its contents, her inheritance money, the earnings from her books, her computer, her horses and three paintings (the fox picture, *Gone Away*, and the self-portrait of the artist—to her vet, Dr. Harry Hastings. The only condition was that he live in the house and that the paintings by John Trentham always be hung together. It was a new will, signed only two days before her death. It was rumored that Harry fainted at the reading and had to be revived by his brother John.

It was also well known that her solicitor, old Mr. Stokes, was bringing a copy of the will to her home on the morning of her death. He never recovered from the shock of hearing that she had been murdered. He had a heart attack and dropped dead. "It was all he talked about," said his wife, testifying at the inquest. "Going up to the house and seeing those paintings. He said there was something he had to warn her about them. There was some kind of danger that he'd remembered. He didn't tell me what is was, but he wanted to see her. She made such an impression on him, she did." She burst into tears.

Alison's death and Jack's wild accusations were an event made for media coverage. It had everything they could have dreamed of—a well-known author, a murder, an angry husband, a lover, and an inheritance. And if it wasn't Harry that Jack had seen in the garden kissing Alison, what had Jack seen that had driven him mad? Research by the press into Jack's background showed that prior to this incident, he had been a completely sane, successful businessman. Toxicology tests proved there were no drugs in his system. The media speculations, fueled by gossip, then moved on to include apparitions and ghosts, which grew ever more outrageous as the days went by.

Lisa watched as every night on television they played and replayed scenes of Jack's outbursts and Harry's obvious distress. The photos that Jennifer's fiancé, Alfred, had taken of Jack threatening Harry at the book signing were played over and over.

Harry looked thin and pale, a broken man who blamed himself for everything. The television showed his haggard appearance as reporters repeatedly asked, "Dr. Hastings, what was your relationship with Mrs. Simons? Were you lovers? How does it feel to be a millionaire overnight? Did you know you would inherit her wealth?" He, who had always rescued others, was now in need of being rescued himself.

It was raining the day of Alison's funeral. Lisa arrived very early. She wanted time to sit quietly and remember her friend, but she was surprised to find that the little church was already filled with people and flowers. Every seat was taken, and those who didn't have seats had to stand outside in the rain. She was glad she had brought an umbrella, just in case. She wondered what Alison, who had thought of herself as being so alone, would have thought of being mourned by so many.

The Hastings family, including Harry, his father, and his brothers and their wives and children, arrived in a crowd. Hastily, under the shelter of umbrellas, they made for the front door of the church. Only Fred, Harry's dad, saw Lisa. His face lit up as he greeted her, clasped her cold hands in his large ones, and said, "So glad you're here, lass. Come in with us, and sit next to me." He had always liked Lisa. She was a real Trentham, just like her dad, with whom he had spent a lot of time on the town council. Lisa was a strong and capable woman, and what was even better, with two children, both boys, she was a proven producer. Harry needed sons. Julia, Harry's first wife, he had never liked, and Alison, he had always thought of as being much too high-strung for his boy. He had always approved of arranged marriages and strongly regretted the days of their passing.

Surplices swaying, the choir, followed by the rector, who looked more gaunt than ever, walked up the aisle. The sound of the organ playing an opening hymn filled the air, and the service began. Lisa's eyes filled with tears, as the rector reminded them all of the goodness of Alison's life, of her large donation to the church for a new roof, that man born of woman has but a short time to live, and last, of the evils of possessiveness and greed. When he finished speaking, there wasn't a dry eye to be seen; women and men alike wept openly.

Alison was to be buried in the churchyard that afternoon. "I'm glad she'll be sleeping with her family," said Fred to Lisa. "These newfangled cremations—they don't seem right somehow." There was a final hymn and a prayer, and then as everyone began to leave, John and Philip, Harry's brothers, closed in on Harry, supporting him with their presence and their strength.

The Nightingales were opening their home that afternoon for the reception. Now that the service had ended, everyone wanted to shake hands with the reverend and thank him for his eloquence. Then they drifted in the direction of their cars. Most were looking forward to getting together with the Hastings family at the Nightingales'. The press, having left behind one or two to video everyone leaving the church, had already made a beeline for their vehicles. It was obvious to Lisa that they were going to be at the reception before anyone else and that Harry was going to be besieged by them.

His dad noticed it too. This was not what his boy needed. He gasped, as suddenly he felt a sharp pain in his chest. He had to do something quickly. He folded Lisa's arm in his and walked toward his son, saying, "Look, Harry! Look who's here."

Lisa took her cue. "I'm Lisa T. Jones—Lisa Trentham Jones, Alison's best friend," she said. "You and I—we were at school together. Your dad and mine were good friends. Please, I need to talk to you privately. I have two horses that sort of belong to both of us." She turned briefly toward Harry's dad and mouthed "Thank you." Then she said, "Come on, Harry. Let's get out of here. It's going to be a zoo at the Nightingales'. We'll go to the Three Brothers Café."

Harry looked absentmindedly at this determined, tall, well-built young woman with short, dark curly hair. He was too grief-stricken to argue. He went with her like a lamb.

The Three Brothers Café was almost empty, most people being at the reception. Lisa and Harry sat at Alison's favorite table by the window. Watching the street as she had so often watched it with her friend, Lisa swallowed the lump in her throat and blinked back the tears in her eyes.

Harry said, "I don't think I can eat anything. I feel sick."

Lisa ignored him and ordered a pot of tea and fish and chips for two. "Harry," she said, "did Alison tell you all about Colossus's win at Wetherby?" Without waiting for an answer, she began to tell him about the day she and Alison had spent at the races. When the meal arrived, it smelled so good, and Harry was so interested in what Lisa had to say, that without thinking, he began to eat.

"What a day that was," Lisa said. "Alison was beside herself with excitement. We arrived early, ostensibly to get a good parking place, but I think Alison was too excited to sleep the night before. When they brought the horses into the paddock, Colossus stood out from all the other horses. He looked magnificent, his black coat shining, but he stood there with his head down. I thought he looked depressed, and I remember Alison saying, 'He thinks he's going into the starting stall. He's in for quite a surprise. He's going to have fun today,' and she patted him gently.

"The thing was," Lisa said to Harry, "none of us knew if he'd run at all, let alone jump the fences. Alison had picked out some silks for the jockey, dark green with diamonds for the shirt and a yellow cap. 'Green as grass,' she'd said. 'That's what Colossus is, and yellow for me, my favorite color.' She had a long chat with the jockey, and all I heard her say was, 'Please do not whip him.'

"Anyway, all the horses jogged past the stands, and Colossus was very slow, peering at everything, looking for the starting stall. But after the horses—all twenty of them—had cantered down to the first fence to remind them why they were there, Colossus suddenly put his ears up and became more interested. When the horses were all lined up behind the tape, and the starter gave the signal, he hesitated. We both thought he was going to be left behind, but then, off he went like a rocket. He cleared the first fence by a mile, almost jumped his jockey out of the saddle, but after that he handled it like a pro, and he won it easily. I'm not sure who was more ecstatic—me, O'Reilly, or Alison," Lisa said.

*****

"He did it! He did it!" Alison shouted, laughing and talking all at once.

"Would you like to come and see a horse in my barn?" O'Reilly asked. "She's just giving me fits, and won't run at all."

"First things first," Alison said, and away she went to lead the horse into the winner's circle. Then there were the photographs, and then she had to cash in her tickets. Lisa saw she had a handful of them. *I don't know how much she bet,* Lisa thought, *but a lot, knowing Alison. And she's just glowing. This must be the happiest day of her life.*

Once Colossus was settled, O'Reilly drove Alison and Lisa out to his training stable to look at a mare he was worried about. Alison seemed impressed because everything was so open—all the horses could see each other, and O'Reilly said he owned the farm next door and grew his own feed. He even had some sheep he liked the horses to see. "Keeps them interested; no time to get bored," he said. "Jimmy will bring Colossus home later, after all the tests, but I want to show you that mare before it gets dark." He brought out the mare—a beautiful creature but nervous and thin. The whites of her eyes were showing, and she tossed her head up as high as she could.

"And is she saying anything to you?" O'Reilly asked Alison. "The owners really want her to win. Her sister is a stakes winner, and she should be able to go the distance. They paid a lot of money for her."

Alison looked at the mare carefully. "Don't you go listening to Lisa, O'Reilly. Horses do not talk to me. Colossus happened to come along. I happened to like him, and we got lucky today."

From the expression on O'Reilly's face, Lisa could tell he didn't believe one word Alison was saying. They watched as Alison stepped back from the mare and the groom walked her up and down the aisle. Finally, Alison said pityingly. "You know, not all horses like this racing life; they're not all meant to race." She ran her hands over the mare's body, pressing here and there and massaging. The mare found her touch calming and began to relax. "Some of them are so nervous, they can't settle down. It's the way they're bred, and then, of course, you could shorten the distance. Try her at six furlongs. Let her relax. Let her enjoy herself. See if she can win a couple of easy races and maybe the owners will retire her as a broodmare."

"That's what I keep telling them," O'Reilly replied, and then he cheered up. "I'll tell them you recommended it. That'll work, especially after they hear about Colossus."

Then Alison made the man laugh. She told him that he had one brown gelding "with honest eyes," who definitely spoke to her. She thought the Nightingales would really like him. "If you ever decide to sell him, I've promised him a retirement home in the country," she said. After that, O'Reilly wanted her to see his best three-year-olds. "I have them in a separate barn in the back," he said. "They're going into training—I think the world of them all."

Alison looked at them, but there was only one she fancied, and she immediately made an offer, subject to a vet check and X-rays. "Come on, O'Reilly," she said. "I've made you a fair offer. After all, what do I know about racehorses? You're bound to prove me wrong on this one."

"I don't want to prove you wrong on any of them, but why that one?" he wanted to know. "Did he say anything to you?"

Alison just laughed at him. "It's a gamble, O'Reilly. Win or lose, it's just a gamble for me, like it's a gamble for you."

O'Reilly grinned. "Maybe you'd want to come to Ireland with me, look at more horses, and gamble a bit more."

*****

Lisa sat back in her chair and smiled wistfully at the memory. "It was on the way back to Roystone the next day that Alison told me of her plan," she said to Harry. "She asked if I wanted to go in with her, that she had an idea for that twenty-five acres. Now that she was getting a divorce, she said, she wanted to do something practical. She wanted to open a training stable with O'Reilly. She said it could be for racetrack lay-ups or conditioning but that we needed to buy that mare. O'Reilly had showed Alison her pedigree, and she was royally bred—a quality mare. Alison insisted that if she ever came up for sale, we should make an offer on her. 'Her owners haven't a clue,' Alison told me. She was sure we could retrain her.

"So, Harry, I did go in with her. Alison gave me the money. I bought the two horses in our names, and I have them at my place. There were a couple of others of O'Reilly's that she fancied. She told me which ones and how much she intended to offer on them after they were started. There was one that had the same pedigree as Colossus, and she wanted him to keep as a stallion, if he had any talent on the track. You know what she was like, Harry. Once she had an idea in her head, she just went ahead with it."

"*Them?*" he asked. "I thought she just bought one."

"Well, she ended up with the one that wanted to retire—for the Nightingales. I'm putting in some training on him to make sure he's safe before I show him to them. Harry, Alison and I bought and sold horses for years, and we never lost a penny. I don't think we will this time. Think about it. She was so full of life, so happy in that last month before that murdering bastard killed her." Lisa fought back the tears. "The horses are her legacy to us."

"I don't know," Harry said wearily. "Alison wanted me to go in on Colossus with her, but I turned her down—money, you know. Then she gave me a half interest and a check for half his winnings at Wetherby. I had no idea she had bought another racehorse. When I first met her she looked so … fragile."

"Oh, that was Jack. He had her scared to death of everything. He was such a bully. I begged her to leave him years ago, but she wouldn't. I don't know what she was more afraid of—him or being alone. Did you know Colossus won at Clonmel too? You know, being alone was the only thing that woman feared. She took a big chance with that horse, and it paid off."

Harry thought of Alison as she was on that last day—so full of life, she had conquered all her fears. He thought his heart would break. He loved her so much, and he had promised to always be there for her. He had let her down. "But I know nothing about racing horses, let alone running that kind of business," he said.

"You don't need to worry," Lisa said. "O'Reilly is longing to go in with us. I'll run the business, and we'll need a good vet. That's you, Harry. That's what Alison had planned for us all. Let it be her legacy. Please. And that little mare is running in a claimer next week. We must bid on her."

"She left me everything … everything." He looked absolutely overwhelmed. "Lisa, I need your help. Alison has a safe in her study, and her publisher, some chap called Beaky, wants me to open it. Her computer's in it, and he's convinced there might be an outline for another book on it. He keeps phoning me and phoning me and he won't take no for an answer. Let's go up to the house right now," he said. "I must do it soon, and I can't face it on my own."

21

Lisa drove slowly through the town and up the narrow, winding road to the house that stood at the top of the hill. Harry put in the new code, and the gate swung open. As they stopped at the front door, Harry reluctantly opened the door of the truck. A flock of crows, resenting their presence, cawed noisily and rose in a black cloud from the sycamore trees.

How sad the house looks, thought Lisa. *Sad and lonely, as though it knows someone it loved is lost forever.*

Harry took out Alison's key and opened the front door. "I feel like an interloper," he said quietly. "This is … Alison's home." His face drained of color, and he started to shake.

"Are you sure you want to do this?" asked Lisa. "We could come back next week."

"Sooner or later, I must do this," he replied.

But Lisa hesitated. Somehow, something about the house made her feel uneasy. "Let's not stay too long," she suggested. "While you open the safe, I'll put the kettle on for some tea."

Harry nodded, rubbing his hands together, "And see if you can find some brandy. Alison has a bottle in one of the cupboards. This house is so cold."

While Harry turned on the gas fire in the living room, Lisa put on the kettle for some tea and found the almost half-full bottle of brandy. She poured a little into two large mugs and drank hers neat, inhaling its warmth.

She found Harry standing in the living room. "Here you are, Harry. Get this down," Lisa said, her teeth chattering. She handed him a strong cup of tea, made stronger by the brandy. "Oh, this house is so sad and so miserable," she said. "Well, here's to you, Harry Hastings. Long life and happiness."

"And here's to you, Lisa Trentham Jones. Long life and happiness to you too. It's been a terrible few weeks. I miss her so much."

"I miss her too, Harry. She was my best friend. Best friends, always and forever, we used to say." And then she said thoughtfully, "Do you remember when we were at school? I was teased so much because of you."

"Because of me?"

"Yes, because of the old saying: 'The house on the hill will be haunted until a Trentham marries a Hastings.'"

He replied sadly, "Not much chance of that in my lifetime. I'll never meet anyone else like Alison. I remember now that the kids chanted it at us. How I used to fight when I was in school."

"Did you, Harry? Because of me?" Lisa replied, beginning to flirt with him a little. When they were in school, she had always thought him an absolute doll, with his blond hair and blue eyes, but he had been going with Julia then. "And now you have a reputation for being such a kind and gentle man." *What am I doing?* she wondered. She was divorced, and after two husbands, both losers, one of whom she was paying alimony to, she had promised herself she was through with men.

Harry was looking at *Gone Away*. "Lisa, what do you think Jack really saw that night?" he asked, struggling to speak, a lump in his throat. "I keep thinking, over and over, about what he said, about seeing a man kiss her. It wasn't me, so who was it?" Harry remembered kissing Alison that same afternoon and involuntarily, he wiped his mouth with the back of his hand and took another sip of the hot tea. And then he remembered Alison on that last day, how different she seemed, and he thought about his two dogs. He would have believed Jack's statements to be pure fantasy except for the dogs. "Why didn't the dogs bark?" he said, as much to himself as to Lisa. "Why didn't they protect her? Why did she stipulate that none of the paintings are to be moved?" Now he took a gulp of the hot tea laced with brandy.

"I don't know," Lisa said. "She never did talk to me about them. Are you to keep them just as they are?"

"Yes, these two and the one upstairs in her bedroom."

"May I go and look?"

"Be my guest," Harry said. "I ... I can't go up there yet. I'll go empty the safe." He walked into Alison's office, opened the safe, took out her computer and a collection of papers. Then, feeling cold and depressed, he sat down heavily on the big couch in the living room, carefully placing the computer and papers next to him. He couldn't face reading any of them. He'd let the solicitor take care of that.

Lisa had poured Harry another cup of the tea before climbing the winding stairs. She remembered all the times she and Alison had run up and down these stairs as children, all the times they had looked for ghosts of long-dead Forsters under the four-poster beds. She remembered sleeping in one of the beds and thinking how creepy it was; she remembered the ghost stories with which Alison had loved to scare her. What an imagination her friend had. Filled with curiosity, Lisa looked in the bedrooms. They were empty now; she supposed that Jack had taken with him everything he considered to be his. And then she walked into Alison's bedroom. She could scarcely believe that Alison would never ever be there again, laughing and sharing stories with her.

The third John Trentham painting was hanging on the wall behind the door, and Lisa looked at it with disgust. *What did Alison see in this picture?* For some reason that Lisa could never fathom, it was Alison's favorite. There had always been something about that fox that bothered Lisa—the way it looked with its snarling teeth as it held down the dead rabbit.

"See any ghosts?" Harry asked her on her return.

"Not one," she replied. "But then, Alison and I looked and looked when we were kids, and we never saw any then either." But Lisa thought, as she re-entered the living room, how different it looked. The light was softer somehow. The room was warm. In fact, the whole house was warm. *It must be the gas fire*, she thought. It was amazing how efficient gas fires could be.

"You know this house has a reputation for ghosts," Harry said. "I asked my dad about it, but he couldn't remember exactly, just that the house had been haunted for years. Alison told me there was a ghost in the linen cupboard. Beth and I looked, but we couldn't find anything. And then there's this." He took a ring out of the pocket of his jacket and placed it in Lisa's hand. "Look at the painting," he said. "I swear the woman is wearing one just like it. The last time I met Alison, she was wearing this ring. My family says John Trentham gave it to Elsie Hastings when they were engaged, and even though she married James Forster, she kept it. It was called the 'blue water.' Alison said it had been given to her in a different lifetime."

"She is wearing a similar ring," said Lisa, examining both rings closely. "You can just see it, very small. Do you think it was this ring?"

They were standing close together comparing the rings, when suddenly the lights flickered and dimmed, and they heard a door slam upstairs. Lisa looked up and clutched Harry's jacket. "Oh, my God! I thought I saw something behind you!" she shrieked. "And what has happened to the lights?"

"Perhaps this house is haunted," Harry muttered. More comfortable now in his familiar role of rescuer, he put his arm around Lisa. She was standing so close to him that his senses were overwhelmed. "Lisa," he whispered. "You are Lisa? Oh, you are Lisa aren't you?"

Lisa froze. "Of course, I'm Lisa," she said. "Who else could I be?"

But Harry, swaying slightly his eyes fixed on hers, said, "Oh, my love Alison, Alison," he groaned. And his arm around her waist tightened. Now both arms were around her, and he held her close, ignoring her hands that tried to push him away. "Alison," he said and inhaled deeply. "Alison, the feel of you close to me—I've missed you so. I thought you were dead … dead. Not dead anymore, my beloved Alison. Now it is I am who am so cold. Help me!" he cried out, and he shivered violently. Staggering, his knees buckling, he fell onto the couch knocking Alison's computer and papers to the floor with a crash.

Lisa, trying to remain calm, felt his forehead. "You're not cold. You're awfully warm. I wonder if you're running a fever."

Harry muttered, "You know something, Alison? You look just like the woman in the painting!"

"Don't say that, Harry. I don't look in the least bit like her. I'm Lisa. Don't you recognize me? What happened just now? I saw something? Did you see anything? What is happening to us?"

"Alison," he muttered, gazing at her. "I love you so much … love her … so very much," he said. He wanted to think about what was happening to him, to puzzle it all out, but suddenly, he felt so tired. "It must be the brandy," he said, rubbing his hands over his face. "I can't stay awake. It's been days since I've slept."

Lisa looked at him in despair. The situation was deteriorating. She should never have agreed to come to this house. She had to get help. Desperately, she tried to think of a way out but couldn't think of anything. She wasn't sure if Harry could even walk to the door. "You'd better rest," she said. "Here's a cushion. I'll get you a blanket, and I'll call your brother right now." She picked up Alison's computer and papers and took them into the kitchen with her, intending to put the kettle on for more tea. She dumped them on the table, dropping some of the papers on the floor in her haste to call John, but the phone was dead—and so was her mobile phone, which was odd, as she had charged it that morning. "I'll try again later," she called out, but on her return, she found Harry curled up on the couch, fast asleep. She felt his forehead and his hands. He was still much too warm, but he was sleeping, and that was the best thing for Harry right now.

Maybe I should get him a blanket, she thought. So she walked quickly back up the stairs. This time she noticed that the door of the linen cupboard was open. Had it been open when she was up here earlier? She sniffed. There was an odd odor of … was it turpentine? She'd tell Harry about it later, when he woke up. She pulled out a large wool blanket from a shelf and tucked it under her arm.

And then, without knowing exactly why, Lisa walked again into Alison's bedroom. Some instinct she couldn't resist told her to take another look at the fox painting behind the door. She sucked in her breath as she stared at it. Where was the fox? Now there was only the tree trunk. How big and hollow it looked as it curved and stretched on forever and forever into darkness. Somehow, it was tempting her. Calling her. She felt as if she could walk right into it! She blinked, and then, just as suddenly, like a snapshot taken by a camera, the scene changed—the fox picture was as it had always been.

Feeling hypnotized, Lisa leaned forward and touched the surface of the painting, thinking perhaps she could put her hand through the canvas, but it was solid to her touch.

Shivers went up her spine as she had the sudden sensation that someone was looking over her shoulder. She whirled around, but there was no one there. Then she caught sight of her reflection in a mirror, with the reflection of the fox painting quivering behind her. She shivered again, and clutching the blanket, she ran back down the stairs as fast as she could.

Downstairs, nothing had changed. It was all so quiet. Harry was still asleep, his face flushed. She covered him with the big wool blanket, and he moaned. *We must leave!* she thought wildly. *We must get out of this house!* If only she could reach Harry's brother John, he would come and rescue them, but again, she was unable to reach anyone on her mobile phone. Every number she called was dead—there wasn't even a ring tone. The kettle began to whistle, and the sound made her jump. To steady herself, she made more tea, and then she turned on the radio. Oddly, on all frequencies there was only the sound of static.

Perhaps if she could get Harry to the car, they could get to the reception. She opened the front door and ran to the car, but the engine wouldn't start—it wouldn't turn over. The battery was dead, like the battery in her mobile phone. It was dusk now. There was not one light to be seen anywhere. The rain had stopped, and the only sound was that of water dripping from the eaves. The sky was clouded; the trees were dark. She felt as if she were suspended in time, the only one left alive in the world.

She found she was breathing as fast as if she had run a marathon. "Get a grip, Lisa," she said to herself. "You'll have to wait this out." She closed and locked the front door and leaned her back against it to gather her wits. Then, deliberately and calmly, she settled herself in the chair opposite Harry, with a small glass of brandy. *There's nothing I can do,* she thought. *I must be calm for Harry's sake.* She looked at him with compassion, thinking what a sweet man he was. This time, Alison had been lucky in love.

As she stared at the two paintings and sipped the brandy, it grew darker and darker outside. In spite of the darkness outside, the room glowed with a golden light, and Lisa could still see both paintings clearly from where she was sitting. *Is there something special about this hunting scene?* she wondered. It was a woman jumping a fence on a chestnut horse, and a man on a black horse was waiting for her on the other side. Harry was right—the woman was wearing a ring. If the woman were wearing the blue water, was she Elsie? And if she were Elsie, then was the man waiting for her John Trentham? The man in *Gone Away* and the self-portrait were like two peas in a pod.

She remembered the description that Jack had given of a tall man with dark curly hair. *Could it have been John Trentham that Jack saw with*

Alison that night? Was it John Trentham who was kissing Alison with such abandon? How could Alison have betrayed Harry for someone dead for over 150 years? Surely it was impossible!

It was hard to believe that anything so incredible could have happened … yet Alison wanted the paintings to be left as they were on the wall. Why? These paintings were just oil paintings, yet … Lisa knew she had seen the fox painting without the fox. What had she seen? She shuddered. What strange force could have caused Alison to abandon her life? With Harry as her lover, she had everything to live for. What had she experienced that made her change her mind?

Restless with her thoughts, Lisa walked to the French doors, opened them, and stepped outside. The garden looked ordinary and bare. And then, although it was a garden in winter, and there were no leaves or flowers, she inhaled a scent—there was just a trace of the scent of old roses in the air.

She had to admit to herself that she was disappointed. Part of her had been so hoping to see what Jack had seen, hoping to see Alison again, one more time. *Oh, Alison, I miss you. I'll always miss you.* Death was so final. Tears filled her eyes, and now it was she who felt alone.

Then, she saw something—and it was something that stayed with her, close to her heart, for the rest of her life. It was all so much like a silent film. She saw the Dog and Duck Inn and the hounds and the horses. And there was Alison and a man—that must be John Trentham—was throwing her up onto her horse, sidesaddle. She was smiling, leaning down, and saying something to him. One of the huntsmen was blowing a horn. And then, just as suddenly, the scene faded away, so that Lisa couldn't see clearly what was happening. Already, it was over. Then all was in darkness again.

Lisa stepped back into the house, closed the doors hard, and locked them tight, refusing to admit to herself what she had seen. Harry must have heard the doors closing for he awoke with a start. She heard him call out, "Are you still here, Alison?" When she joined him, she saw that he was shivering violently. Lisa felt his forehead—he was burning up. Again, she tried to reach Harry's brother John on her mobile. Why didn't he answer?

As she walked into the kitchen to pour herself another cup of tea, she saw the papers scattered on the floor and bent down to pick them up.

One caught her eye. It was a note addressed to Alison from her father. Quite without meaning to, she read:

> *My darling girl,*
>
> *Do not hang the three paintings, Gone Away, the Fox, and the small self-portrait now owned by Dr. and Mrs. Nightingale on the walls of this house—ever. If you do, the ghost will walk, and you, Alison, are too like Elsie to be safe from him.*
>
>

I love you my little bird,

Dad
>

So that was it! Now Lisa understood what was happening. Immediately, she went into the living room and removed the self-portrait from the wall, intending to carry it upstairs. She wrapped her arms around it but found she couldn't carry it next to her body. Her flesh immediately began to crawl from its contact. She ran up the stairs in the semi-darkness and grabbed a sheet from the linen cupboard. This she wrapped around the painting, and thus protected, she managed to carry it up the stairs to the linen cupboard and lean it against the wall. She placed a blanket over the sheet, and then she closed the door firmly behind her and set off slowly down the stairs, legs shaking, clinging to the banister.

"Alison," Harry said to her on her return, "you're white as a sheet. Anyone would think you had seen a ghost. Are you wearing the ring?"

Lisa looked at him. Thankfully, he was sitting up. She felt his forehead again. It was damp with sweat but it was cooler now. Yes, she had done the right thing with the painting. The spell was broken. Of one thing she was certain—Alison had betrayed this man's trust with another lover, John Trentham, and Harry must never know the truth!

"Harry, can you get up? We really should go to the reception," she said. "They'll be expecting you."

"I can't. I'm so tired, Alison," he said, feverishly clinging to her hand. "Let's just stay here. I can't face all those people right now and all the photographers. I just want to sit here with you, and be quiet, and hold your hand."

Did he lose his mind? Lisa wondered. If necessary, although she dreaded the thought of it, she would put the other two paintings in the linen cupboard that night.

She went into the kitchen and called his brother one more time, and this time there was a reply. She heard John's anguished voice. "Harry, is that you? Dad had a heart attack at the reception. He's gone. It was over so quick. We've been trying to reach you for hours. Where are you?"

Lisa tried to explain everything, but John interrupted her.

"Lisa, can you help? Please take care of Harry. He and Dad were always so close. There's nothing he can do here. If he finds out right now … We'll be there as soon as we can." His voice broke down.

Lisa's heart sank. The only bed in the house was the one in Alison's room, and she was not going into that room again if she could help it. She sat on the couch with Harry. It was going to be a long night.

"Don't leave me, Alison, will you?" he repeated over and over. Then he said, "The ring! The ring—are you wearing the ring?" The light in the room shifted, and shadows passed over the painting, almost making the horses move.

Oh, Harry, so many terrible things have happened to you, Lisa thought. She sat beside him now, first holding his hand, and then holding him closer, reassuring him. She had no idea what had happened to the ring. "You're going to be okay. I promise I'll take care of you now," she said.

And as they sat together, talking quietly, they grew drowsy. The room was so warm. They were so comfortable. All was so quiet; the light in the room so golden. It was as if they had received the blessing of the house and the spirit that inhabited it. They fell asleep until morning and awoke in each other's arms. When they awoke, the blue water was sparkling on the fourth finger of Lisa's left hand.

*****

Eighteen months later, Lisa Trentham Jones was married to Dr. Harry Hastings. The Reverend Durham recited the ceremony. Lisa was radiant. She was wearing a dark blue velvet riding habit with a blue hat to match. Her wedding rings were the blue water and a plain gold band.

Harry, smiling, looked the complete gentleman, with top hat, white breeches, and red jacket. "I owe you my life, Lisa," he had said more than once as he struggled to recover his sanity. The diagnosis by his doctors was a complete breakdown, caused first by a painful divorce, second by the murder of Alison Simons, and last by the sudden death of his father.

Lisa nursed him through all his fears and panic attacks at her home and then in the house on top of the hill. For months, he was convinced that Lisa was Alison, come back to him. "Don't leave me, Alison," was his terrible cry.

"I'll never leave you, Harry," Lisa replied. "I promise."

There were at least six hundred guests at the wedding ceremony, including his family, her family, the mayor, and the town council. The town was so very grateful for the three John Trentham paintings that Harry had loaned to the museum.

Lisa had attended the dedication ceremony, in memory of Alison Simons. "You see," she told the paintings. "See where it got you," but in her heart she knew that paintings live forever, that she was but mortal, and such forces as she had witnessed live on.

On the day of the wedding, crowds of well-wishers filled the streets, hoping for a glimpse of the bride and groom. The Nightingales opened their home and grounds for the event. "One last celebration," said Dr. Nightingale to his wife. "Let's do it right. Let's make it a big one." Lisa and Harry were married in the formal garden, in 1850s costumes, on horseback. Harry was riding Bear. Lisa was riding Captain, sidesaddle. Lisa's two children from former marriages, both boys, were the ring bearers. Harry's two girls, who had decided that their new life did not suit them and who had begged to come home, were bridesmaids. Lady, as the maid of honor, organized them all. When Lisa threw her bouquet into the air, it was Lady who caught it, and she refused to share.

Champagne flowed like water. The food, catered by the Dog and Duck Inn, was plentiful. The event made the local television, the front page of the local newspaper, and the national television, eclipsing even the news of the opening of the new Roystone Shopping and Conference Center next to the racecourse.

When the groom dismounted from his horse, lifted down his bride, and kissed her enthusiastically—kisses that she returned—there were cheers and whistles of approval from the entire crowd of well-wishers. Then, to everyone's surprise and delight, Harry's brother John drove up in an elegant carriage pulled by two matched gray Welsh ponies. Harry handed his bride into the carriage and then took the reins, and he and Lisa drove away into their future, amid showers of confetti.

"Well," said Mrs. Crocket to Mrs. Pollock. "Did you ever think it would end like this?"

"Never," that lady replied, all teary-eyed. "Never in a hundred years."

There was a new sign next to the wrought-iron gate of the house at the top of the hill. It read "Forster, Trentham, and Hastings: Training and Racing Stable."

The land sighed. The contract was fulfilled.

All was as it should have been so many years ago.

ABOUT THE AUTHOR

Lin Harbertson was born in Yorkshire, England, where her family owned an old home, complete with four-poster beds and ghosts. Lin now lives in Virginia with her husband, dogs, and ponies. *Doorway through Time* is her first adult novel. She previously published several children's books under the pen name Lin Edmonds, about the adventures of Patric the Pony. She presently is writing the sequel to *Doorway through Time*.

CPSIA information can be obtained at www.ICGtesting.com
Printed in the USA
BVOW071752170413

318426BV00002B/202/P